THE NEXT MARGARET

THE NEXT MARGARET

BY
JANICE MACDONALD MANT

Mosaic Press
Oakville-Buffalo-London

Canadian Cataloguing in Publication Data

Mant, Janice Elva, 1959-
   The Next Margaret

ISBN 0-88962-573-5

I. Title.

PS8576.A57N4 1994   C813'.54   C94-931077-8
PR9199.3.M35N4 1994

Published by MOSAIC PRESS, P.O. Box 1032, Oakville, Ontario, L6J 5E9, Canada. Offices and warehouse at 1252 Speers Road, Units #1&2, Oakville, Ontario, L6L 5N9, Canada and Mosaic Press, 85 River Rock Drive, Suite 202, Buffalo, N.Y., 14207, USA.

Mosaic Press acknowledges the assistance of the Canada Council and the Ontario Arts Council, the Ontario Ministry of Culture, Tourism and Recreation and the Dept. of Communications, the Government of Canada, for their support of our publishing programme.

Illustration by Susan Parker
Design and typesetting by Susan Parker
Printed and bound in Canada

MOSAIC PRESS:
In Canada:
   1252 Speers Road, Units #1&2, Oakville, Ontario, L6L 5N9, Canada. P.O. Box 1032 Oakville, Ontario, L6J 5E9
In the United States:
   Mosaic Press, 85 River Rock Drive, Suite 202, Buffalo, N.Y., 14207
In the U.K.
   John Calder (Publishers) Ltd., 9-15 Neal Street, London, WC2 H9TU, England

ACKNOWLEDGEMENTS

I would like to acknowledge the Alberta Foundation for the Arts for its support of this project. I would also like to thank my friends who read various drafts; my cabal of mystery students who supported me, my husband Colin, whose vows include proofreading; and my mother, who has always believed in me.

DEDICATION

This is for my girls: Madeleine and Jocelyn.
Mommy loves you.

Intoduction

I was getting used to a lot. The basement suite that had at first looked so dark and dingy was finally beginning to seem cozy; I was starting to make inroads on the campus that stretched, mazelike, over a couple of square miles; and I'd even braved the bus system out to the behemoth of a shopping centre that the city fathers seemed so inordinately pleased about. One thing I didn't think I'd ever acclimatize to was the cold.

The wind that had blown me into town stripped the leaves from the trees two weeks later. The rain that had whipped down all day was threatening to turn to snow come evening. The optimists I met were promising me an Indian summer, but I wasn't banking on it. It's been my experience that it doesn't pay to trust the promises of folks that aren't in control. The realists were buttoning their jackets to the chin.

I bought a down-filled coat at the Army and Navy. I looked about as fashionable as any well-dressed member of a polar expedition. It did nothing for my appearance, but it warmed my bones. What was I doing in the middle of a western winter? An M.A.

Bill had laughed when I'd told him my plans.

"An M.A. in Canadian literature? Don't give me that shit about expanding and developing your potential. You're just running away from the real world."

"The real world is barely keeping me in Hamburger Helper," was my witty rejoinder.

That was not exactly true. For one thing, I don't eat Hamburger Helper. For another thing, I wasn't doing too badly as a freelancer, times being what they were. When the jobs came along they usually paid pretty well, and I was getting my share of the ever-decreasing piece of pie that was allotted to freelance writers. The trouble was, I was getting tired; tired of the push for deadlines, tired of the grubbing around producers and editors for work, tired of never feeling financially secure enough to refuse a job. I just wanted to come in out of the cold for awhile.

That's not exactly true either. I loved the idea of coming back to university, this time on my own terms. I've always been a nut for research; I count libraries and archives among my favorite places. I'm the sort of person who reads whole pages from the dictionary on the pretext of finding out where to hyphenate "reification".

Besides, I finally had a thesis topic.

I know, I know. You're thinking that, with this kind of start, I'm hardly qualified to organize a garage sale, let alone a thesis. Allow me to explain that it is common academic practice to leave the Introduction till the last, so that you'll know what you've actually said when you get to finally saying it. Clear as mud, right? All right, we'll compromise. I'll start over, and you keep going.

Chapter 1

I'd been doing a stint of book reviewing when I'd run across Margaret Ahlers' first novel. By the time the weekly ran my rave, my opinions had been both preempted and confirmed by the Globe and the New York Times Book Review. The confirmation almost made up for my "also ran" status.

One for Sorrow, a first novel by Margaret Ahlers, is a work to treasure by a writer to be reckoned with. The playfulness with which she handles the shifting sands of a seemingly transparent relationship is matched by her artful and deceptively simple use of language. To say that Canada has found its Iris Murdoch would be reductive. Ahlers is a new voice, a fresh voice, and a welcome voice.

I couldn't have said it any better myself. In fact, if I could have said it at all, maybe it would be me that was writing for the New Republic instead of Anne Tyler. All I knew was that I wanted to write about this writer. I wanted to immerse myself in her style and delve into the intricacies of her imagination. And, although I knew it wasn't fashionable academic practice anymore, I wanted to find out everything I could about her.

Immersing and delving were no problem. Finding out anything about Margaret Ahlers was a different matter. All the dustjacket said was, "One for Sorrow is Margaret Ahlers' first novel. She is presently at work on her second." There was no chatty bio and no picture-with-pipe-and-typewriter on the back cover. There wasn't even a dedication.

Little things like this do not deter the truly dedicated snoop. On the grounds that I was planning a feature story, I called MacKendrick's.

"MacKendrick and Sons. How may I help you?"

It is my experience that publishers' receptionists are usually more interested in what Krystle will be wearing on the next episode of Dynasty than they are in their company's spring list, so it never fails to puzzle me when they sound so tony on the phone. Maybe they've got a message taped to the switchboard.

"Hello, I'm from the Gazette. We're planning a feature on one of your new writers, and I was wondering whether you might help me out with some biographical details."

"Oh, you'll want to speak to Ms. Dubeckie. Just a moment, I'll see if she's available."

MacKendrick's was a class establishment; I didn't get any canned music in my ear when she put me on hold. I bet the phone even sounded like a subdued doorbell when it rang.

"Ms. Dubeckie can speak with you. I'll transfer you through."

"Hello?"

"Hello, Ms. Dubeckie?" I began my spiel from the top. I was beginning to believe in the feature myself. Ms. Dubeckie was obviously buying it. What publisher can resist free publicity?

"I'm certain we can accommodate your request. What author was it that you required information on?"

"Margaret Ahlers."

"Margaret Ahlers?"

The surprise in her voice made me wonder just how big MacKendrick's spring list was.

"Yes, Margaret Ahlers, the author of One for Sorrow?"

Ms. Dubeckie's voice became distinctly chilly. Any more frostiness and she was in danger of falling into cryonic suspension.

"I'm afraid we really cannot divulge personal information about our authors."

"Well, perhaps you could give me her address and I could deal with Ms. Ahlers directly."

There was a long pause. I could almost feel the coolness of her hand over the mouth piece as she conferred with someone else in the office. It was as cool as the voice that eventually came back on the line.

"If you care to write to Ms. Ahlers in care of our address, we will forward her mail to her."

I thanked the ever-so-helpful Ms. Dubeckie, and replaced the phone on its cradle. I wasn't quite sure what to do next; while my bluff seemed fine over the phone, I wasn't so sure about committing the idea of a mythical feature to writing.

I was still mulling over Ms. Dubeckie's mysterious about-face, when the phone at my elbow rang. This was my day for talking to book companies. My friend Garth Johnson, whom I sometimes refer to as "my publisher" when I'm trying to impress people, had a job for me. The next thing I knew, I was up to my armpits in memories, ghosting the autobiography of one of the last riverboat pilots to ply the waters of the Athabaska. Freelancers can't be choosers.

In the six months that followed, my curiosity about Margaret Ahlers was relegated to the dustiest corner of my mind. I was too busy embellishing the rather meager facts and sifting through the outrageous fictions it had taken Jimmie Cardinal seventy-two years to create to worry about a mysterious Canadian author. Most of Jimmie's stories involved buxom lady bartenders. The bits about the bars had a certain ring of truth to them. Maybe it had something to do with the background ambience on almost all the tapes. I could almost smell the spilled beer emanating from the terrycloth tablecloth as Jimmie rambled through my headphones. I'm not a real fan of taverns, so it surprised me that I was getting rather fond of the old codger. As a token of my affection I left in Lucy of McMurray and Jennie from Fort Chip. It was the least I could do for the friend I'd never met.

By the time River Man hit the stands, I'd almost forgotten about Margaret Ahlers. Almost.

Chapter 2

I'd cut my ties with the Gazette by the time *Two for Joy* came out, so I had to shell out the $22.95 myself. While I have no compunctions about buying books, I usually can resist the urge until they appear in paperback. Not this time. My need to read Ahlers' second novel was substantially greater than my desire to retrieve my suede jacket from the cleaners or my compulsion to renew my subscription to The Malahat Review. Besides, I had to absolve myself of the sin of covetousness, and the only way to do that was to buy the book. I raced home with my purchase, feeling like a bulemic with a quart of butter-scotch ripple.

It was stunning. She'd made good on all the promises of her first book and then some. Where her first novel had been dazzling, this one was strong and commanding. The voice was sure and powerful. She played with the reader - coaxing and teasing; sometimes infuriating, but always alluring. *Two for Joy* felt like Pynchon and Thurber and Stoppard and Calvino all rolled into one. Ahlers was amazing.

I knew what I had to do. I phoned a friend of mine, Sharon Tindle, who was working as a sessional lecturer. She's a sessional because all the tenured positions for those specializing in Restoration Drama are held by bee-pollen-eating professors who will never die. Sharon taught three courses a year, published her requisite articles, and was kind enough to lend me her library card occasionally. She was also my only remaining contact with academe. I made an appointment to "do that lunch thing" with her on the following Tuesday. She knew I wanted to pick her brains about something; but she didn't mind. I would be picking up the bill.

"We should do this more often," Sharon said, forking down her shrimp cocktail. "I haven't seen you since you needed all that history on the Great Lakes."

She was referring to a project I'd been hired to do a while back. I'm not much of a history buff, but that seems to be where all the money is these days, especially if you want to squeeze any funding out of the government.

"Actually, I wanted to talk to you about universities, Sharon."

"Really? Is this an expose, or are you doing another government study?"

"Neither. It's absolutely personal. I want to go back to school, and I thought you might have some ideas about where I should apply."

"You've got to be kidding. You, back at school? I thought you couldn't wait to get out the last time?"

"It's different now. There's a project I want to work on, and. . ."

"Don't tell me, I know. I heard about the budget cutbacks at the CBC." I wasn't sure why she was looking at me with such pity; she's only on an eight-month contract. I resisted the urge to point this fact out; I needed her, and antagonizing her was not the way to ask for a favour. I swallowed my set piece on the joys of the gypsy life of freelancing, and tried to muster a grin.

"Well, yeah, that's part of it; but the main thing is, there's this writer I want to work on, and she's new so there's bound to still be plenty of scope for thesis material, so I thought why not." I was treading on dangerous ground; in Sharon's field it was hard to squeak out another article on *The Beaux' Stratagem*. Luckily, she didn't seem to notice the potential gaffe; I guess she was too caught up in imagining me in plaid skirts and knee socks.

"Randy Craig, M.A." she mused. "Who'd have thunk it?" She roused herself from her disbelief and prepared to give me her full attention. "Who's this wonderful writer?"

"Margaret Ahlers," I said. Just hearing myself say the name out loud gave me a tingle. I knew I was on the right track.

"Ah, the Great Canadian Hope," Sharon nodded a little too smugly for my satisfaction.

"Have you read her stuff?" I demanded.

"Really Randy, if Bakhtin can get away with stopping at Dostoevsky, I see no reason to justify myself by curtailing my literary studies with John Gay." Sharon sniffed. "I've heard she's quite spectacular," she condescended.

"From who? Is anyone working on her already?" I felt like I was fourteen again, lusting after Duncan Worthington, and hearing that he'd asked Kathy Dekkar to the Valentine's Dance.

Sharon noted my proprietary jealousy with a smile.

"Well, I've seen a couple of articles on her, I think. From some woman out west. Quill, I think, or Quinn. Quite recently. Well, I suppose they'd have to be, wouldn't they? She is fairly new on the scene."

I was getting confused.

"Who's new? Ahlers or this Q woman?"

"Ahlers. No, this woman - I'm sure it's Quinn, yes, has been around quite awhile. I think I've met her, or heard her give a paper at any rate, at the Learneds a couple of years ago." Sharon looked at me over her wine glass. "You know, Randy, if you're so het up on working on this Ahlers, maybe you should look into working under Dr. Quinn."

I could almost hear myself purring. This was the sort of information I'd wanted. I knew I could count on Sharon. She promised to find out where Dr. Quinn was on faculty, and to look up the articles she'd written on Ahlers. I could have hugged her. Instead, I cheerfully picked up the tab.

Sharon called me a week after our expensive lunch.

"I've photocopied those articles and popped them in the mail." Sharon is egotist enough to never identify herself on the phone. "I've also located Dr. Hilary Quinn, Associate Professor of English, acknowledged expert to date on the works of that great Canadian novelist, Margaret Ahlers. Anyone I've found that knows her speaks well of her. A real nose to the grindstone type. Seems this Ahlers coming along has done her a world of good. The only other submissions I can find by her are various Notes and Queries. If you ask me, her criticism's a bit stolid; still, it's sound." It must be all those years of lecturing; Sharon's capacity to hold forth without taking a breath was really impressive. Finally I managed to get in a word.

"That's great, Sharon. Thanks so much. I owe you. So, where do I go to study with this woman?"

Sharon's tone took a nose dive.

"I had a feeling you were going to ask that," she said.

Chapter 3

The University of Alberta is a wonderful institution. It boasts a fine library collection of Canadian literature, from the first edition of The History of Emily Montague to the complete Fiddlehead Poetry Books, with perhaps the best collection of English-Canadian drama in the country. Its English Department consists of over sixty full-time faculty, with a strong graduate program. It also happens to be located in Edmonton, which I understand is "very lovely in the summertime."

There's a joke about preparing yourself for an Edmonton winter. You're told to stick your head in a deep freeze and repeat to yourself, "Yes, but it's a dry cold!" At least, I thought it was a joke when I first heard it in the middle of September. A few weeks later, I wasn't too sure.

Being a Forces brat, I'd done a longish stint in Lancaster Park as an adolescent, and I figured I was on speaking terms with Edmonton as a city. The university was another kettle of cod, though. All I remembered was the Jubilee Auditorium next to the residence towers, and a really boring piano recital I'd been taken to in Convocation Hall. My date had been Howard Davies, a pretentious Grade niner with illusions of adequacy. The place had been full of Italians who yelled "Bis, bis" after every number. As I recall, the rest of the world had been at a Three Dog Night concert. That's what you get for being Ms. Nice Guy.

Anyhow, I was unprepared for the campus when I arrived on the scene. For one thing, it'd be hard to tell where the university officially started if it weren't for the "welcome" signs posted along the perimeters. None of the buildings matched. Low, older buildings hunched alongside sandstone towers; brick facades gave way to plate-glass; it seemed like the central principle of design had been lifted from one of my grandmother's crazy quilts.

Assorted science buildings sprawled anywhere they wished; Biological Sciences, Agricultural Sciences, Medical Sciences, Clinical Sciences, Earth Sciences, Dentistry, Pharmacy, Forestry. Physical Education had staked out its territory in the west corner of the campus, virtuously distancing itself from the carcinogenic fast food outlets. One of their newer gyms was shaped to represent a huge pat of butter. Perhaps they hadn't yet heard about cholesterol.

Maybe it was just my imagination, but the social sciences, humanities, and fine arts all seemed huddled together along the eastern front. All the buildings here were attached by enclosed walkways to a long structure named HUB. It was a residence/cum/shopping centre/cum universe unto itself that stretched for three city blocks down the eastern edge of the campus, from the central transit stop to the river's edge. Stairwells placed at regular intervals on either side took you up to a bubble-roofed, enclosed pedestrian mall. HUB boasted a grocery, a drug store, a laundromat, a bar, several restaurants and food kiosks, a secondhand bookstore, some clothing boutiques, bank machines, knicknack shops, a video arcade and several coffee lounges. Student apartments looked out over the mall via colourful cupboard-door shutters. It reminded me of a high-tech medieval street.

So much for the static scenery. The daily kaleidoscope of human beings was amazing. At ten minutes to the hour, every hour, a swarm of colour whirled through the corridors, down the sidewalks and across the covered walkways. HUB seemed to be the Piccadilly Circus of the U of A, if not the New World. You probably could run into everyone you knew if you could bear to sit there long enough. People-watching in HUB was rather entertaining in a macabre sort of way. The natives did their best to live up to their surroundings. Student "uniforms" had certainly changed since I'd last played co-ed. The days of a pair of jeans and a clean T-shirt had seemingly gone the way of the brontosaurus. I felt like a peahen must when the boys are in town as I milled about with the preppies, punks, and members of other assorted fashion sects. There's something disheartening about seeing someone half your age with half your yearly budget on her back. I took to slinking my coffee back to my office until I'd had a chance to upgrade my cords and cottons to flannels and cashmeres.

My office was a refuge and haven in all the possible senses of the words. It was decorated with two desks, two bulletin boards, two bookcases, two garbage cans, one filing cabinet and a door that locked. At first sight, the second desk scared me; I've never been much good at sharing anything, let alone air space. After meeting Maureen, however, I realized that there wouldn't be any problem. She spent all of two hours a week in the office, during which time she counselled bewildered students. The rest of the time she spent in the library or at home, beavering her way through a massive reading list for her candidacy exams. I never did quite figure out what she was studying and her dissertation title, "Architectonics in the Faerie Queene" didn't provide me with many clues. To tell the truth, I didn't spend many sleepless nights wondering about Maureen. She was pleasant enough when I saw her, but most of all I loved her for her absences. The office quickly became my fortress.

I have always been in favour of the second Law of Thermodynamics. Entropy, which most people equate with chaos, to me denotes the contrary. Anywhere you look, you're bound to find at least part of what you're looking for. Perhaps I've only adopted this philosophy as a defense for my sloppy habits. It could be a chicken and egg question. Whatever the case, my office soon took on the outward manifestations of the organized turmoil that was my mind.

Of the turmoil of my mind there was no solution but ther were plenty of reasons. Three graduate seminars a week, teaching a course which met twice a week, a bibliography course which met one hour a week, and a "teaching a freshman English" course which took up another hour a week. During

the breaks I was trying to fit in a little eating and sleeping.
Selfish of me, but then, I'm like that. I stopped trying to count
sheep, and instead, at the end of a long day I'd try to remember
reasons why I'd thought university would be better than the
real world. I'd usually drop off after Reason 1: Not having any
money means not having to balance your chequebook.
Welcome to U of A, Randy Craig.

On top of this I was trying desperately to find and
waylay Dr. Hilary Quinn.

Chapter 4

Almost the very first thing I had done after arriving at the Department of English was to sit down and write a letter to Dr. Hilary Quinn. In the letter I explained my fascination for Margaret Ahlers, made flattering remarks about Dr. Quinn's articles on the topic, and expressed a desire to meet with her and perhaps work under her. It was tripe, of course; I'd found Quinn's articles rather stodgy, and in my fantasies I could see my thesis shooting through the ozone hole to become the definitive statement on Ahlers, but I couldn't say any of that. So I lied. Nonetheless, it was a convincing letter; I've had a lot of practice writing for the government.

It took me three weeks to convince myself that my epistle hadn't been inadvertantly buried under departmental newsletters. Dr. Quinn wasn't answering. Who knows; maybe she'd written for the government, too. I wrote another letter. This one was humble; I was an M.A. candidate searching for a thesis advisor. Could I make an appointment to see her? Still no answer. I was beginning to wonder if I'd somehow managed to insult her without knowing who she was. Had I bumped into her shopping cart in the Safeway? Had I barged into line in front of her in the Student Union Bookstore? Was she the woman who had glared at me when I collapsed onto the last free benchspace in HUB? If I'd had time to put my mind to it, I probably could have worked myself into a complex.

Luckily, I didn't have time to worry about my own sense of self-worth. I'd just finished marking a set of first-year essays and was starting to organize my thoughts for a presentation in my Canadian Lit. seminar. It was tough slogging. Everyone in the seminar seemed to be taking a different critical stance, and as far as I could tell, none of the tacks had anything to do with whether you "liked" the book or not. I was desperately trying to sort out New Criticism (which was considered passe) from narratology (which had little to do with "what" and an awful lot to do with "how"), deconstruction (sort of like decomposing, but less smelly) from structuralism (a stance I had previously thought peculiar to engineers and architects), and how to tell a Leavisite from a Marxist (I think it has something to do with how they cross their legs). Some of my fellow students were watching my flounderings with contemptuous sympathy, but it didn't really bother me all that much. When you've been around the block as many times as I have, you get kind of a kick out of being called "naive".

I'd begun to get my sealegs around the department, and so felt comfortable enough to sit in a corner of the Graduate Lounge with my books and a cup of coffee from the drip machine in the corner. Maureen was offering grammatical advice and Kleenex to the under-50% crowd from her class, so it was impossible to get any work done in the office anyway. Snivelling might be good background music for Chekhov, but it did nothing for my appreciation of Susannah Moodie.

I was immersed in Upper Canada conundrums when the voice broke through the soundscape.

"You're Randy, aren't you?"

I bit off my stock reply, "Maybe, what did you have in mind?", and looked up, nodding, into a pair of the biggest green eyes on the planet.

Still nodding, I took in the rest of him. He had blond, curly hair arranged in the style someone's mother would call a mop. His long, angular body was covered in a faded plaid shirt, a brown jersey that had seen better days in 1962, and a pair of blue jeans. His scuffed hiking boots looked like he wore them for the right reason. The only thing wrong with the picture was that a knapsack hung from the hand where his guitar case should have been. I twitched my head to clear it; this was U of A, not the Mariposa Folk Festival. Wherever we were, I was in heaven. I've always had a thing for musicians, even reasonable facsimiles thereof.

"I'm Guy," the dream spoke. "May I sit down?"

As I slid over on the couch to make room, I realized I was still nodding like one of those Made in Taiwan papier mache statues with the spring in its neck. I stopped, feeling heat start to move outward from behind my ears. Guy didn't seem to notice. He was too busy folding himself onto the couch. He stuck one leg up on the coffee table, and grinned.

I needed an original gambit.

"I haven't seen you around before." Even to me, it sounded flat. I think that's why I became a writer; I need the safety net of a second draft.

"No, I just came in to get my mail. I'm working at home this year." He then went on to tell me all about his scholarship, his study of wordplay and game theory, and his work schedule as if he were the most interesting topic anyone could come across. The trouble was, given the options, he was beating C. Parr Trail's chatty sister all to hell. Maybe that's what they meant by "naive reader".

"What about you?" The green eyes turned on me like headlights on a rabbit. The tips of my ears started to get hot again.

"Oh, the usual. Three courses, teaching, and fighting to find a supervisor."

"What's your area?"

It was as if Ali Baba had just hummed the first few bars of "Open Sesame". Out poured everything: my interest in Ahlers, my attempts to get hold of Quinn, my inability to catch her in her office.

"Well, she's not around till Christmas, is she?" Guy inserted at the tail end of my diatribe.

"What do you mean?"

"She's on some sort of half-leave, I think. Hold on a sec, I'll check it out."

He unwound himself from the contortions of sitting in a human-sized chair and loped out the lounge door. He was back in a matter of minutes.

"I've just asked in the office. Dr. Hilary Quinn is on a half term, unpaid leave until January. They're collecting her mail for her because she didn't want it forwarded. Her teaching schedule next term is Tuesdays and Thursdays, with an evening class Wednesday nights. Makes for nice long weekends, don't you think?"

I was amazed. I was about to ask how he'd found out all that information in so little time when I caught sight of those eyes again and made the connection. The office staff are all female.

"Thank you for taking the time," I managed to say before I was silenced by the shaking of his head.

"Oh no, 'thanks' doesn't cut it as a reward."

"What does?" I found myself smiling. I could say that abject arrogance amuses me, but who would I be kidding?

"How about pizza? There's a great place a couple of blocks away called Tony's. Draft beer, thick crusts, gingham tables, candles dripping out of basketed bottles. What do you say to seven o'clock?"

I felt more like a cork on a wave than an immoveable object, but there was no doubt at all about Guy being an irresistible force. I felt myself nodding again.

"Great. I'll see you then." He was halfway out the door when I asked him, "By the way, how did you know my name?"

He turned and grinned again.

"Oh, I make a point of being well informed."

I had no trouble believing him. Taking a gulp of ice-cold coffee, I managed to bring down the blush he'd left behind.

Chapter 5

You'd think I was dressing for my Senior Prom for the amount of time it took to decide which sweater to pull over my cleanest jeans. I was still feeling unsure as I pushed open the door that had Tony's woodburnt in script across it. Guy waved to me from a table in the back corner of the nicely dim restaurant. As I approached the table, he smiled with an approval that made me thankful I'd chosen my rainbow pullover that looked like it was knit out of pipe cleaners. It had cost a whole fifteen minute radio segment (first draft) at ACTRA rates, but it was worth every penny. I wear my clothes like armour, and in this sweater I always felt invincible.

"Isn't this place great?" Guy poured me a glass of beer from the pitcher on the table. "I found it the second week I was here, and it's been my hole in the wall ever since."

Tony's was a nice place. I abdicated to Guy's decision once I'd made sure he hated anchovies, and took the place in as he ordered. There were enough patrons scattered around the room to put some trust in the food, but nobody close enough to intrude on our dinner. Music was playing softly on a stereo; I couldn't quite put a name to it -- Telemann or Mozart, I thought. The waitress left the table, and I felt Guy's attention turn back on me. There was something unnerving about the way he looked at a person, as if he was calculating checkmate six moves ahead.

"So why grad school?" he shot at me suddenly.

"I thought I'd explained, I want to write a thesis on Margaret Ahlers, and this seemed like the best place;" I felt my voice fading as he shook his head slowly.

"No, I don't think so," he said. "There's something about you that doesn't jive with the whole student set-up."

I was starting to do a slow burn.

"You don't? What am I then, a spy?" I wasn't sure whether it was his omniscient attitude that was nettling me, or the fact that he'd seen through my pose. I wasn't all that sure I belonged in academe, but I didn't think it showed like some neon mark of Cain.

Guy seemed to think it was funny.

"I can see it now; Comrade Randy reports that they use a nine point grading system at U of A. No, I didn't mean that you were here for some ulterior motive -- it's just that I sense that you're on some sort of mission, rather than just jumping through hoops to get extra letters at the end of your name. Missions aren't that common in the English Department, in case you hadn't noticed."

"I'm surprised you're not in the Psychology Department putting your interpersonal skills to better use." My words sounded archer than I'd meant, and I immediately regretted them as I saw Guy's smiling face take on a mask-like quality.

"Sorry," he muttered, "I wasn't meaning to pry."

"Of course you were," I said, treading water, trying to get back to the comfortable island I'd found myself on moments before. "It's not that I mind, either. Actually, it's quite flattering to be the focus of attention. It's just that no one likes to feel absolutely transparent to total strangers."

"I wouldn't call us total strangers," Guy interjected. "Total strangers do not share Tony's Bacon, Cheddar Cheese and Green Pepper Specials."

"I'm sorry, I was wrong. You belong in Law, not Psychology." I gave him a mock salute with my beer glass. "I suppose that makes us kindred spirits of a sort. You're an attorney in scholar's clothing, and I'm some sort of moonie in search of a degree."

"This isn't fair," Guy pouted. "Where I come from, I'm usually allowed to be the life of the party." He gave me another quick, penetrating glance. I wondered if he had a license to use those eyes. "I was serious before. You're after more than an M.A., aren't you? You can tell me; I won't let on to the rest of the flock."

"Would they even listen to the black sheep?"

"Who's the psychologist this time? I guess you're right, though. I've never been sure whether I chose the role, or adapted to it once it was thrust upon me." He reached across the table and gave my hand a quick, impulsive squeeze. "I'm glad you turned up, Comrade. It's been lonely here at the top."

The pizza arrived just in time to keep me from making a nasty remark about arrogance. As I chewed through the mass of molten cheese, I was glad I hadn't. It struck me that Guy had been speaking the truth about himself. I'd snuck a peek at his dissertation proposal in the file in the mailroom earlier in the afternoon. On a first read through it had seemed very scholarly, with references to Huizinga and Nabokov and Barthes. There was something about the tone, however, that made me give it a second read. I couldn't be sure, but I had a sneaky feeling that Guy Larmour was making a game out of game theory. Anyone that could pull that off, in what struck me as a rather conservative department, had every right to preen. Guy's words broke into my thoughts, and I realized that I hadn't been the only one doing research that afternoon.

"I picked up *One for Sorrow* at Forrest's this afternoon, but *Two for Joy* isn't in paperback yet, so I took it out of Rutherford. I assumed you wouldn't need the library copy?"

Startled, I assured him that I had my own copy.

"Why so surprised?", Guy laughed.

"I just didn't think you'd be so interested in a relatively new Canadian author."

"Well, to tell you the truth, as far as I'm concerned Ahlers herself can go hang. What I am interested in is a relatively new Canadian grad student, and the way to any student's heart is through her research."

"What about her stomach?"

"The pizza was the alternate strategy," Guy laughingly admitted.

"Is everything a game to you?" I asked, with more curiosity than condemnation.

"Pretty much. In the long run, it makes it easier to stay clear-headed if you keep the rules in mind."

"I sense that you take play pretty seriously."

"Indubitably," he remarked. "In fact, as you get to know me better, you'll find that I take everything pretty seriously."

"Well, as far as the research goes, while I appreciate the gesture, I have to warn you that I'm rather jealous of my work."

"Point taken. I'll just read the novels so that I can follow what you're saying. I promise not to butt in." Guy crossed his heart.

I laughed at his little boy seriousness.

"I mean it, Guy. Stick to the pizza gambit. I have never felt a need to discuss my work, and I'm not about to start now."

In a few months' time I was going to have to eat my words, and they didn't have the flavour of a Tony's Special.

Chapter 6

In a way, I was glad that Dr. Hilary Quinn hadn't been here to greet me with open arms in September. I was barely treading water with the work involved in the coursework for the degree. In the Green Book, which houses all the rules and regulations of the department (except for the ones that apply), it said that the expected time for completing an M.A. was one year. So far, I'd heard of two people that had done it. I'd come across about thirty frantic individuals, juggling writing for courses with reading for courses with teaching freshman courses with trying to come up with a thesis topic and an advisor. In this instance, I had the jump on them. I'd already drafted three different thesis proposals.

At the moment I was leaning toward a study of regionalism and the land in Ahlers' novels. I'd once heard Robertson Davies talk about the fact that Canadian writers were sitting on some the oldest land, geographically speaking, in the world and that, being sensitive, this had to make a difference to their writing. I suppose he was talking about the Canadian Shield, but I figured it might hold true for western writers, too, the way the topsoil had been blowing away this year.

There's something very strange about Canada the country. My father maintains that North America should have been divided vertically rather than horizontally. He says it's because westerners understand westerners and Torontonians are more like New Yorkers than other Canadians, but personally I think it's because he could then golf professionally in California without a green card. He might be right in spite of himself, though. For all the years I had spent out east, I had to admit I was starting to feel at home again.

I'd decided to explore the regional quality in Ahlers. It made sense as a project for two reasons. First of all, I hadn't really noticed a particular regional flavour to the novels on a first reading, although they were deliberately set in the northwest. Secondly, no one had written about Ahlers and regionalism yet. There were a couple of articles appearing here and there about the two novels, but so far the mysterious Dr. Quinn was still the so-called expert on the topic. I'd tried to winkle an address for her out of the secretaries, but it seemed that not even Guy's charms could work miracles. Quinn hadn't left an address. I decided that hounding her wasn't the best way to begin a working relationship anyway, so while she continued to hover in the ether, I devoured books on regionalism while I wasn't cramming for Canadian Lit. or Narrative Studies, or skimming through the Twentieth Century Novel, or checking the Norton Guide for ways to teach war poetry. In fact, I'd almost completely forgotten about Hilary Quinn until two things appeared in my pigeon-hole to remind me. One was a memo informing us we had two weeks to submit our approved thesis proposals. The other was a copy of Margaret Ahlers' third novel--*The Children of Magpie*.

Chapter 7

I rushed through my thesis proposal with a codicil attached explaining how I hadn't been able to contact Dr. Quinn. The Grad Chairman was understanding and approved it conditionally. *Children of Magpie* was burning a hole on the edge of my desk, but I'd promised myself I wouldn't touch it until I had my exams marked. It was December 16th before I had the grades tucked up in their yellow folder and could relax into the yuletide spirit.

Christmas spirit on campus had dribbled away to nothing by this time. The department party had been held on the final day of classes and exam time was marked only by excess activity in the photocopying room. By the time my grades were in, most everyone had faded away to sunny shores or family hearths. The secretaries were still smiling in the general office, but I found the atmosphere in the Humanities Building too dampening to stick around. I moved my notes and Ahlers' new novel back to my subterranean hovel (read: basement suite), bought a mickey of white rum and a litre of dairy-made eggnog, and settled in to cocoon.

Guy had left a message on my phone machine, something about skiing Whistler. Since my idea of winter sports is to burrow into woolen underwear and hibernate, I wasn't even sure of which direction he'd gone. The pang of realizing I wouldn't be able to give him his present on the actual twenty-fifth was lessened by the thought of the new novel on my lap. I snuggled under an afghan and cracked the spine the way they taught us in grade six, just to prolong the anticipation. In a matter of pages, I too was on holiday.

Magpie seemd to be a throwback to the style of the first novel. Whereas *Two for Joy* had been the exploration of a weird symbiotic relationship of two women, this novel was again a one-hander. The character, Isabel, would often share the role of narrator, mostly when looking back on her life, or forward into her dreams. The present of the novel was dealt with in a limited omniscient. It seemed to be playing with the concept of actions of the past informing and shaping the present. The futuresque dream sequences had prophetic qualities that recreated the past. It was hard to explain. It was like watching Pinter's *Betrayal* and then fusing it with its mirror image running forwards again, except that the characters all knew what would happen this time. I wasn't up on contemporary writers well enough to know whether anyone else was writing like this, but whatever the case, I was sure glad Ahlers was.

I closed the covers reluctantly when I reached the end. It had taken me two days to read it. I set it on the side table, made myself a grilled cheese sandwich, ate it, and walked around the apartment picking things up that I'd strewn about during the last two days. I found myself staring blankly out my kitchen window at the snowdrift in the window well. I couldn't shake myself out of the novel. I felt like an iron filing near a magnet. With a sigh, I threw myself back on the couch and picked up the book.

I was about a third of the way through it for the second time when the phone rang. It was my parents calling from Australia to wish me a happy Christmas. They were giggling a bit giddily because they'd been up half the night trying to figure out the time zone equivalents. Their Elderhostel course was going well, they'd met up with several of the people they'd met in Spain the year before, and they were shipping me a sheepskin vest.

"I hope you're not spending Christmas alone, Miranda," my mother was saying. She always used my full name when

I became an object of concern to her. It would be too costly both in terms of phone bills and worry to try to explain that being alone didn't bother me. It was an old argument between us, anyhow. My mother tried to unshackle herself from her fifties mindset, but she still couldn't fully accept that I might choose to remain single. I assured her that I was going out for dinner with a friend. In a way I was. I could take *Children of Magpie* with me for pizza.

They promised to send postcards of Ayers Rock and rang off to throw a shrimp on the barbie.

I spent the rest of the week doing laundry, organizing three lectures on *Pride and Prejudice*, and finishing a short paper on Frederick Phillip Grove for my Canadian Writers seminar.

On December 29th Dr. Quinn phoned. We arranged to meet on January 3rd.

Chapter 8

Dr. Hilary Quinn was not a bit like I'd been picturing her for the previous six months. I'd had visions of this rather frail, older woman with her hair in a bun. Don't ask me why; maybe my brain's casting director lumped all bookish types- -professors, librarians, authors, bookstore clerks--into one. All I know is that Central Casting had to do a massive reshuffle when the office door swung open.

Dr. Quinn was taller than average for a woman in her early forties. She had shoulders I'd have killed for, the Joan Crawford kind without the pads, and short dark hair that resembled anthracite with a few strategically placed veins of iron running through it. She wore a large red sweater over a black and red tartan skirt. I was going to have to fire my casting personnel; Dr. Quinn was all together the quintessential professor.

"Miranda Craig?" There was something in her tone that kept me from explaining my preference for Randy. I used Miranda, the name on my birth certificate, only when necessary, like on university applications. Randy was a better name to publish under, more androgynous. I'd rather be mistaken for a man, which often worked in my favour, than spend time fighting the preconceived notion of Shakespearean naif.

Quinn smiled as we shook hands, but her face didn't light up. Fine by me, I figured. If cool and reserved was the way we were going to play it, I could do the popsicle with the best of them. She motioned me into her office and closed the door behind me before resuming her place behind her large desk. I had a quick sense of bookcases on each wall, floor to ceiling, two massive sideways filing cabinets, a few plants on the window ledge, a personal computer in the corner and some very nice paintings before Dr. Quinn focused in on me again. She caught me with my eyes on a painting of a lake that seemed to have about seventeen distinct horizons as part of the design.

"Interesting work, isn't it? It's a McNaught."

"I beg your pardon? I didn't catch the name."

"McNaught. Euphemia McNaught. A Peace River Country artist. Student of the Group of Seven."

"She's very . . . engaging," I stumbled. Art has never been my strong point. I feel as awkward discussing aesthetics as I would declaiming a wine as having an "unpretentious yet amicable bouquet." I was hoping Quinn was going to let me off the hook and she did.

"You're rather older than I expected from your note."

This had me confused. Had I said anything age specific in my note? I hoped she wasn't referring to my rhetorical style. I was just beginning to bridle when she continued.

"I take it you are working toward your Master's?"

I breathed an inward sigh of relief as I nodded. I'd forgotten that aspect of the career academic, the sort that teethes on Milton and has their PhD. at fifteen. Of course I was older than Quinn had expected; how could she imagine starting an M.A. at thirty? She'd probably been in the biz for at least six years at my age. I plastered on a placating smile.

"I took some time out to travel and pay off my Student Loans."

Either irony was wasted on Dr. Quinn or I was losing my touch. She nodded in a businesslike way and folded her hands together on top of her desk.

"So, why don't you tell me what you'd like to work on? I gather it's something to do with Margaret Ahlers."

This was it. I took a deep breath and began to ramble immediately. After about five minutes of garbling terms like "regionalism", "space", "terrain" and "inner reality" my diatribe trickled to a halt. To my surprise, Quinn looked interested.

"I see. You want to tackle the metaphor of place and belonging in Ahlers' fiction within the context of Canadian regional dictates. Not a bad idea. There seems to be enough scope for an M.A. thesis there. What graduate seminars are you attending at present?"

We went on to discuss my timetable and schedule, plotted a time to meet on a semi-regular basis, and ended up, forty minutes later in the same position we had started in. In the doorway, shaking hands. I bounced down the hallway toward my own little cubby hole at the other end of the building. Things were rolling right along.

Or so I thought.

Chapter 9

If I had expected to bask at the feet of the master, I changed my expectations in a hurry. While Dr. Quinn allowed for a meeting every second week, she didn't ever seem too het up over it. She'd sit and listen to my "research so far" and, occasionally, she would nod or say "Hmmm." I never did learn to translate those "hmmms;" they didn't appear consistently near either triumphs or mistakes. After about an hour and a half, Quinn would unfold her legs, which she had wrapped around each other about three times during the course of the meeting, and clear her throat. This was my cue to stand up and say, "I'll see you next time."

She never marked anything except grammatical errors on any papers I handed to her. I narrowed it down to two possibilities: either I was a genius or there was something weird going on. Having the self-confidence of a salamander, I proceeded to get spooked.

Guy was not the rock he thought he was.

"Are you sure you've read all her articles? Maybe you've contradicted something she's written."

"Thank you, thank you. This is just what I need to hear. Shall we start humming the Volga Boat Song now, or maybe just go out and hang ourselves?"

"You're getting too worked up about this, Randy."

"Well, I just can't figure her out. One minute she's nice as pie, the next minute she's staring off into space, ignoring me."

"Sounds like a godgame to me."

"A what?"

"A godgame. You know, you are the player, but you don't know the rules. You try to go one way, and the god who is the game master lops off your arm because somehow you've trangressed some unwritten law."

"How could I have known about it if it's unwritten?"

"Exactly! The god toys with you. Like flies to wanton boys and all that malarkey."

"Do you really see Hilary Quinn as a god?"

"It's not what I see, it's what Hilary Quinn sees when she looks in the mirror in the morning."

"Hmmmm."

"What's that supposed to mean?"

"What? Oh, I don't know, why don't you ask Dr. Quinn?"

"Why don't I just order more beer?"

"That's what I like about you, Guy, your priorities."

So there I was. It was mid-March, my seminars were winding down in spirit as the workload increased proportionally, my freshmen were getting more interested in what would be on the final than on the importance of literature in their lives, and people around me were generally going a little crazy.

I had three major papers to submit, one presentation left to do (in the course I understood the least) and a comprehensive exam to set. I pitied my poor bunnies; even I couldn't remember what we'd covered in September. Not only that, I was beginning to believe that my advisor was out to get me. Did I say "other" people were going crazy?

Chapter 10

I would like to take this moment to dispel the myth that all intelligent people have a passionate interest in current affairs. Personally, I only buy the papers for the crossword puzzle and my reviews. I figure that if there is a mass murderer out there, I would rather not think about it. Most of the time the news that affects me personally catches up to me within a few days, and I can usually find the crossword page lying around near a coffee lounge.

This disregard for authorized gossip has occasionally led to embarrassment, but only once to a fight. The fight was with a radio current affairs man who thought I was some sort of imbecile because I wasn't aware of Senate reform. When I told him I hadn't been aware of the Senate in the first place, he lobbied to have me made redundant. So strong were his feelings that he almost had me believing, or should I say, not believing in myself. I bought three papers a day for two weeks, and read them cover to cover. I learned that newsprint makes you filthy if you come within a yard of it. I learned that in this day and age I should try to remember to only come within a meter of it. I tried to pepper my coffee conversation with informed comments about the state of the world, but this only made the current affairs man patronizing. I was despairing of ever getting the news black off my cuticles when I discovered that the current affairs man had never even heard of Scheherazade. I stopped reading the papers.

My mother, out of some abject fear of my being caught without some important piece of news, writes tidbits into her letters. For some reason, it's always the deaths of important people that she tells me about. It reminds me of a comedian I once saw who said his grandmother reads the obituaries every day and then crosses the names out of her telephone directory. I suppose that's what we want to hear about, though; it's comforting to know who's fallen out of the race while we're still in the running.

I didn't have to wait for Mom's letter to hear about this particular obituary. Maureen had thoughtfully left the page on my desk, and Guy came by about twenty minutes after I'd hung up my coat.

"Did you hear?"

All I could do was nod.

"You weren't planning on interviewing her, were you?"

I shook my head.

"Listen, let me buy you a cup of coffee." Guy led me out of the office and down the corridor. I felt numb, so numb that I hardly noticed my knuckles scraping against the stucco of the corridor wall. The architect had obviously had his own ideas about the sex habits of English professors; the hallways were treacherous if not navigated single file.

Guy bought coffee, snaffled a table, and sat me down.

"Here's to Margaret Ahlers. May she rest in peace."

"Oh, Guy. I can't believe it."

"I know what you mean; after all, her latest book came out, what, a couple of months ago?"

"It's not that so much. I guess, really it's because she hasn't become a household word yet. I mean, who even knew what she looked like? There's no signature; no frizzy hair, or moonlike madonna face, or bow tie, or kilt, or wolf smile, or twenty-seven cats. Who was she?"

"That's not part of the bargain, Randy."

"What do you mean?"

"I mean that, unless you're Truman Capote, you don't write a book in order to become a personality. You write a book to communicate what you have committed to the text."

"This is the part where you call me naive again, isn't it? Because I don't care, I think people want to be able to recognize their bards on the street. Movie stars parroting someone else's words are celebrated, why not those who wrote the words in the first place?"

"I suppose you want to know who Thomas Pynchon is, too."

"Damn rights. And I want to meet J. D. Salinger."
Guy snorted. I think he was letting me ramble to get rid of the shock. He probably had seventeen different arguments to prove that the author is insignificant in the true course of events. I stared into my styrofoam cup, trying to divine an answer to the universe. Guy's voice startled me because it was so unexpectedly soft.

"I was sitting in bed reading and listening to the radio when the news came out that Borges had died. The announcer stumbled over his name, it came out something like Georgie Louise Borgia, but I just started shaking my head, because it wasn't true. Borges wasn't dead, he was right there in my hand, with me. I'd been rereading 'Death and the Compass.'"

I looked up at Guy. He was sitting across the table, looking vulnerable and hopeful and so damn nice. The greatest new Canadian voice was silenced, any hopes I might have had for a personal interview were shattered, I felt like someone had taken a cookie cutter and punched it through my chest.

"Guy, get me out of here. I think I'm going to cry."

Chapter 11

My next meeting with Quinn could probably win hands down as My Most Awkward Moment. Try to picture it: two women sit in a small, enclosed place. Both have a vested interest in the work of another woman, who has recently died. Because of social and intellectual restrictions, neither of them is allowed to unveil her mourning face, nor share her grief with the other.

I honestly didn't know what to say. I had mentally attributed to Quinn my grief multiplied tenfold for each article she had published on Ahlers. Since she'd really been churning them out, by rights she should have been prostrate. It said a lot for her sense of dignity that she hadn't cancelled our meeting. I was beginning to think she was made of ice, though. She didn't even mention Ahlers' death.

Finally, I figured I had to say something.

"I caught your interview on the CBC this morning."

Quinn stiffened slightly.

"I thought it was very respectful of her work, very dignified."

"Thank you."

"It seems awful to think there won't be any more."

"I beg your pardon?"

"Any more books. It's tragic to think there won't be any more writing by Ahlers."

"Well, I think the scope of your thesis will suffice on the three texts available."

It was like milking an icicle. I couldn't believe the chill in her voice. Maybe it was true what an old prof of mine had once said, never choose a work you adore to work on for a thesis, because eventually you'll wind up hating it. Did Quinn hate Ahlers' work after all the work she'd done on it? Or maybe, did she hate Ahlers herself? With an impressive lack of tact, I blurted out my next question. "Did you know her?"

Quinn looked at me. I had the feeling I'd hit a nerve somewhere.

"Margaret Ahlers? Yes, I was acquainted with her. The Canadian literary community is, after all, not that large."

Quinn was trying to bluff me somehow. After all, I knew from experience how hard it was to get past Ahlers' publishers to get to the woman. I couldn't imagine her rubbing elbows with Quinn at a wine and cheese party.

"What was she like?"

I wasn't prepared for the sudden blast. If I'd been a cartoon character, my features would have melted under the attack. Now I have a standard by which to measure when people say that someone "laced into them." Quinn laced into me.

"Really, Miranda, this is a literature department. I don't expect to turn a thesis seminar into an excuse for coffee room gossip. Perhaps we should curtail this meeting until you've managed to examine your priorities. Your confusion at this time is perhaps understandable, but that makes it in no way condonable. Good bye."

I collected my notes and blundered out of her office and into the hall. Somehow, in some way I didn't quite comprehend, I suspected I had just made myself an enemy.

Chapter 12

Quinn cancelled my next two meetings with her by leaving terse notes in my pigeon hole. While it made life a little simpler, it also meant I was falling behind schedule on my thesis research. I thought about a change of advisors, but it had me worried. The further you go up the educational ladder, the harder it gets to say, "My teacher doesn't like me." Even couched by terms like "personality conflict," it still smacks of pettiness and failure. Besides, in April everyone is complaining about something.

The halls are filled with people sobbing quietly on benches, people sobbing quietly in bathroom stalls, and the lucky ones sobbing quietly in the privacy of their offices. The unlucky ones did their sobbing on the High Level Bridge. Going crazy in April is common practice in academe; it's the way intellectuals measure the seasons from inside their climate-controlled buildings.

It seemed, though, that Quinn's sudden antipathy to me was not merely a product of my imagination. Dr. Peters, the Graduate Chairman, stopped me in the lounge one day. After looking over her shoulder, she asked in a muted tone, "Is there something wrong between you and your advisor?"

The only inheritance I ever collected from my pioneer ancestors was an inordinate desire to conceal my innermost feelings to strangers. An inordinate desire to clean my house weekly would have probably been more useful. My heritage kicked in as I looked into Dr. Peters' sympathetic face.

"No, not as far as I know. Is there a problem?"

"No, no, just checking," Dr. Peters' voice seemed to precede her nervously out the lounge.

The Associate Chairman of the department smiled at me for the first time the next day, but I put it down to paranoia on my part until Guy cornered me.

"What's happened between you and Quinn?" he asked brusquely.

"I've been telling you for three months, she's weird. Haven't you been listening?"

"I'm talking about lately. Did you two have a fight or something?"

"Not really," I said, recalling Quinn's tightly pursed mouth at our last meeting.

"Maybe what you've said about her has got back to her or something then."

"Wait a second, what do you mean, 'what I've said about her?' The only person I've talked to about her is you, Guy."

"All right, all right, don't look at me like that. I haven't said anything. So we cross that off the list of possibilities. I just don't know. . . "

Guy could be a sweetie. He could also be extremely annoying, especially when holding one of his "conversations for one player." I felt my temper fraying.

"You just don't know what?" I brayed.

He looked slightly startled.

"I just don't know why Quinn would turn down a full Summer Research Assistantship for her M.A. student to help her organize the projected biography on Margaret Ahlers. Didn't you know?"

It's lucky I don't have an alabaster complexion, or it would have shattered as my face hit the floor. I couldn't believe it. No one could be that malicious. No one turns down a free slave, especially not when that slave would be absurdly grateful for the job. What did Quinn have against me anyway?

"You're kidding."

"Sorry, kiddo. That's the buzz among the office staff, and if anyone knows anything around here. . . need I say more?"

"Who's she giving the job to?"

"No one. Says she can handle it, although the powers that be think that an R.A. would help get it published all the sooner, so they offered but the little red hen said she'd much rather do it herself."

"And so she did. Well, that puts the kybosh on my working with Quinn." One glimmer began to shine in my brain. "Hey, with all this happening, maybe no one would question me changing advisors. Peters seemed pretty worried about me the other day. Whaddaya think, Guyo?"

"Can't hurt to try. Watch out you don't get stuck with Martin, though. I think there's a sale on him these days; Carrie just got saddled with him as second reader on her thesis."

"Why would they do that? He's a medievalist, isn't he?"

"Yep."

"But Carrie's working on Norman Mailer."

"Go figure, eh? Maybe they thought there'd be a scatalogical connection."

I winced. Guy in one of these moods could keep you buoyed up for hours if you were in a good mood, but if you were in low gear he could be as aggravating as a telephone soliciter. And about as persistant. I mumbled something about the library, gave him a kiss on the nose, and beat a quick retreat.

I needed time to think about what Quinn had done to me. And to my research.

Chapter 13

I decided that I was damned if some screwball professor was going to rain on my parade. I had a $500 travel grant from Grad Studies to visit the area Ahlers wrote about in her novels. Now I just had to figure out which direction to take.

I felt like Trixie Belden, girl sleuth, as I pored over the novels and the notes I made. Anything that made a specific reference to place I jotted down on a recipe card. If it seemed to be fictional, it went on a pink card. If it was descriptive of area, it went on a green card. If it was bald fact it went on a white card.

So far the only bald fact I had was the section in *Two for Joy* where the two fat American tourists make the hitchhiking girls sit on newspaper in the back seat of their El Dorado and yammer on about the fact that there's no sales tax. It was enough for me. I bought a wall-sized map of Alberta, the only province without sales tax, and set to narrowing my horizons. Hard to do in Big Sky Country, but I had determination on my side. Determination and three ambiguity-laden novels.

Throwing caution and care for my security deposit to the winds, I covered one wall of the kitchen with cork tiles from Canadian Tire. The map was tacked to one side, and various coloured recipe cards kept it company. While the pink ones moved around a lot, the green ones began to seep upwards, consistently above Red Deer, the belly button of the province. There was no mention of ranchland, badland, or scrub, and very few mountains, although they were sometimes mentioned as "looming on the horizon." The descriptions, as far as *A Nature Guide to Alberta* was concerned, seemed to be parkland all the way. I seemed to be heading north and west.

It was the river that clinched it. I'd been sure that the river mentioned was the North Saskatchewan, because, as far as I was concerned it was the biggest river I'd ever seen. Any river that needs a bridge half a mile long to span it rates right up there in my "big" category. That was before I read about the Peace.

To give you some idea of how big this river is let me quote a few facts. In graphs outlining annual water flow, most of the rivers of Alberta are measured in terms of cubic meters. While the graphs occasionally rise to the 200 mark, in July most of these rivers clock in around nil. The Peace River, alias the Mighty Peace, has a graph which is measured in thousands of cubic meters--all year long.

The Peace River Valley is incredibly fertile. In fur trade times, the market garden fort for the district was located at Dunvegan. Today, a Peace River farmstead is twice as far north as a farm in Saskatchewan, and three times further north than a competitive farm in Manitoba. In the summertime the sun doesn't set till past eleven, and while the growing season is short in terms of season, it couldn't ask for more sunshine.

The Peace River Valley area is also one of the last areas opened for homesteading in Canada. There are still people up there who remember building the log cabin let alone the number who were born in it.

So much for external facts. It was the internal correspondence to the Ahlers opus that I was interested in, and I couldn't get that from the *Canadian Encyclopedia.*

On May Day, I rented a car and headed up Highway 43. Now I know how Monarch butterflies must feel when they migrate. I had no real proof, but something at the back of my brain niggled at me when I thought about the Peace River area. I couldn't dredge up the connection, but I knew I was on the right track.

Chapter 14

Even with my general notion that Ahlers had been
writing about the Peace River Country, I realized that I was
headed for an enormous haystack, with only a vague idea of
what the needle looked like. With my luck, if I did find it, it
would be imbedded in my foot.

I stopped for coffee in Valleyview and reconnoitered with
the map I'd found in the glove compartment. The highway
split here, and I had to choose between going north to Peace
River, or west to Grande Prairie. There was another loop from
Grande Prairie, through Dunvegan and Fairview to Peace
River, so it was a choice between travelling clockwise or
counter-clockwise. I seemed to remember some ploy for
avoiding jet-lag wrapped up in these terms, but I figured it
wouldn't really apply to a Dodge Omni. Not wanting to
eliminate scientific principles entirely from my decision, I
tossed a coin. Heads. Grande Prairie.

The only place I've ever seen a live Canada Goose was
in Kew Gardens in London. The incongruity of it surprised me,
but not half as much as seeing swans all over this small,
northern Alberta city. Apparently, Trumpeter Swans migrate
to nest in the lakes around the area, and the city council was
dang proud of it. I passed three statues of Trumpeter Swans
on my way to book into the Swan Motel.

I chose the Swan because it was close to the centre of
town, and was clean and cheap. After a shower, I decided to
stroll down to City Hall to see if I could access the archives

for local history. The weather was sunny and mild, a perfect pre-summer afternoon. The sun was deceptive, though. I'd mentally figured it at three or three-thirty tops, but was greeted by locked doors and a sign which announced that City Hall closed at four. I'll never get used to daylight savings time. I made a mental note to be back at nine the next day, and headed for the library.

I was figuring on finding a local history to occupy my time with until I could check through the registry, but my eye was caught by the bulletin board just inside the doors of the library. There was a large poster declaiming the merits of an Old Time Country Fair being held at the college May 1st. Crafts, artwork, baking, preserves and readings from local poets were promised. I turned back to retrieve my car from the motel. If I was going to find anyone who knew if Margaret Ahlers was part of the local arts scene in Grande Prairie, I had a feeling it would be there.

Whoever sang "it's all happening at the fair" knew what they were talking about. Inside the rotunda a lady with a full scale loom was set up, demonstrating her warp and woof, while a macrame lady was explaining her use of "found art" to complement her hangings. I couldn't imagine just "finding" an entire fan of partridge tail feathers, but who was I to question the artistic process? I moved on. Tables were set up as booths down the hall toward the auditorium. These were laden with cookies, pies, preserves, paper tole and pottery. Grande Prairie, from all accounts, was a crafts mecca.

I headed for the auditorium. On the table at the door was a wooden bowl for loose change, a pile of pamphlets indicating the order of performances within and a few chapbooks, presumably the published poetry of some of the readers. I was leafing through these with one hand, and scrabbling in the pocket of my jeans for some loonies when the lady behind the table spoke.

She asked me if I was enjoying the fair, and if I was from around the area. I answered yes and no as I sized her up. As far as I could tell she was petite and about sixty, but then again she was sitting down and I'm bad with ages. I did notice well-behaved grey hair, a clear complexion, and an ashes-of-roses outfit that coordinated so beautifully it must have been from the Ports Collection. She had a lovely smile, too, which she was displaying to me.

"How did you happen to hear about the Fair?" she asked.

I explained about seeing the poster in the library, and on impulse told her I was searching for some history on a local author. This really seemed to delight her.

"Oh, I'd love to talk to you about your research. I'm a bit of a research buff myself. Perhaps," she glanced at her watch, "we could get together tomorrow sometime. I'm supposed to be judging the preserves right now, and then there'll be the ribbon ceremony and all. Do you have a car?"

I said I did and she whipped a pamphlet from the top of the pile, turned it over, and sketched a brief but clear map to her farm. We arranged that I should "pop by" at about ten-thirty the next morning. She dashed off, leaving a teenager to man her table.

I checked the map, and turned over the pamphlet. After scanning the list of poets and musicians, I decided to keep my loonies in my pocket and make an exit myself. In my opinion, poetry is meant to be kept in a small book tucked into a picnic basket, not declaimed from the apron of a stage to a crowd of sisters, and cousins and aunts. I paused to buy a jar of saskatoon jelly and a small plate of chocolate chip cookies and left the Fair, feeling satisfied that I hadn't been wasting my time. This might not have been how Ackroyd researched Dickens, but then again, they don't have saskatoons in England.

Chapter 15

I turned up at City Hall spot on nine o'clock, and by nine-thirty I'd discovered that there was no record of Margaret Ahlers having ever paid taxes to the City of Grande Prairie. All in all, it wasn't surprising; it would have been somehow too easy to have discovered that she'd run for mayor, but I was disappointed nonetheless. What had seemed like such a great project when I'd applied for the funding was starting to seem pretty thin. My great adventure mode needed a kick in the pants, so I found myself gearing up for my visit to Dorothy Lewis. My inner voice was warning me not to get my hopes up, but my inner voice was the one that got me into this in the first place.

I wasn't sure how the judge of preserves at the fair could help me, but Dorothy Lewis seemed to be my only lead and I clutched at her like a leech on a piece of liver. I found my way to her farm and was rolling down the drive at exactly ten-thirty the next morning.

"Farmyard" is not the word you'd use to describe Dorothy Lewis' landscaped showpiece. I'd seen things like it in *Better Homes and Gardens* and *Architectural Digest*, but frankly, I'd always thought they were airbrushed or something. The driveway of white gravel gave way to flagstones, the kind lesser mortals use indoors. Surrounding the slate slabs was the most amazing border of foliage I'd ever seen. Many of the shrubs and flowers looked familiar and yet somehow out of place. I finally realized that I was looking at a vegetable garden, but not any vegetable garden I'd ever seen before. Carrot ferns bordered purple kale like some sort of Japanese meditation garden; peas frolicked in a vanguard, making way for troops of potatoes, rear lines of corn, and trellises of scarlet runner beans. Equally aesthetic arrangements of onions, marigolds, cabbages, zucchini, and pumpkins dotted the way to the house.

I suspect my mouth was hanging open as I walked toward the tidy woman standing in the doorway of the ranchstyle house. She smiled at me.

"I always felt vegetables got shortchanged when lined up like criminals. They are every bit as pretty as other plants. Why should they look dowdy just because they're useful, too?" She smiled again after this little speech, but I had a feeling I'd been checked out pretty thoroughly by those shrewd eyes. "Well, Miss Craig. I hope you found my map helpful."

"Call me Randy, please," I said, scuffing off my loafers in the doorway. "I had no problem getting here at all, Mrs. Lewis."

"If I'm to call you Randy, which must be a petname for Miranda, that is, unless you're Norwegian, then please call me Dot. Everyone around here does." She started off through the house, with me right behind her. "It's such a beautiful morning, I thought we might have tea out on the deck. Come this way, dear."

What I caught of the house fit right in with my thoughts on the garden. This was one arty little lady. Driftwood for a fireplace lintel, pretty sand layered in a jar for a doorstop, various oils and watercolours on the walls. When we got to the deck I figured out what she had done with the flowers missing from the front beds.

The deck had a half roof, and pots of hanging flowers hung from each rafter--begonias, fuscias, lobelia. Staircase ledges had been set into the two walls, and on every step, a potted flower sat. Sweet peas ran riot on the third wall, which was not a wall at all, but a stretched piece of netting making it possible to peer through the vines and flowers to the sky beyond. Geraniums guarded the stairs to the lawn, one to each side of the three shallow steps. African violets sat in handthrown pots on the table. It was like sitting down in the middle of a bottle of Chloe.

Dot poured the tea. Sure enough, the cups were pottery, and so was the tea set of pot, creamer, sugar bowl and lemon plate. She caught me looking.

"This set was a little project of mine. I was so excited after Harold built me my own kiln that you couldn't pry me from my wheel for months."

I murmured something complimentary. You remember me, the one who shies from comment on art? But I had to admit, I knew I liked the tea set.

"You're not from these parts, are you?"

"No I'm not. What tipped you off? My accent?" I've been told I've picked up a Tarana slur. Personally, I believe it's more of a western drawl, but then I don't have to listen to myself.

"No, your name. I've never heard of any Craigs from around here. Of course, you might have been associated through your mother; what was her name?"

The name Summers did nothing for Dot Lewis either. It seems our Mrs. Lewis was somewhat of an amateur historian of the area, having helped to organize one of those massive books that lists everyone, quarter section by quarter section. While I felt a little snubbed to be so summarily excluded, without even being looked up, I was beginning to think I'd come to the right place. If anyone knew Margaret Ahlers and her stomping grounds, it was going to be Dot Lewis.

Chapter 16

It turned out that "Ahlers" rang about the same number of bells that Craig had for Dot Lewis.

"It's not a local name, I know that. Here, come with me." She led me out of the conservatory patio and back into the cool of the house. In the living room, on either side of the flagstone fireplace, were floor-to-ceiling bookcases. One entire shelf, it turned out, was full of local history books. Dot handed me one, and took another herself.

"Most of them have indices at the back, dear," she informed me. "Let's check if we can find your friend."

"She's not really my friend, she's an author I'm interested in."

"And she comes from around the Peace?" Dot nodded with pride of ownership. "We have a very active artistic community here."

"But you've never heard of Margaret Ahlers?"

Dot smiled.

"Well, you know how it is, I don't get much reading done, except in the winter, and you know how secretive writers can be."

"Tell me about it," I was just about to expound on the secretiveness of Margaret Ahlers when I spotted something familiar on Dot's shelf.

"What about this book?" I pulled a twenty pound tome off the shelf toward me.

Dot gave me a cursory glance.

"*Beaverlodge to the Rockies*? No Ahlers' there, and I should know. That's my old stomping grounds."

It was the cover that had attracted me. It was a wrap print from back to front of a brownish-greenish landscape with about seventy-five horizons. Something about that picture was scratching at my memory like a potshard, and not having the patience that went with that particular feeling, something had to give. Luckily, Dot noticed my concentration.

"Lovely cover, isn't it? It was super of Betty to allow it."

"Betty?" I queried. Dot was amazing, I think she really did know everybody.

"Betty McNaught. You've probably heard of her as Euphemia McNaught. She's a Beaverlodge girl."

McNaught. Of course, it was the same artist as Quinn had had hanging in her office. A Beaverlodge artist. I had the feeling I was getting somewhere.

I flipped to the index. No Ahlers, but then Dot had already told me that. This time, instead of closing the book, I flipped through to the Qs. Sure enough, there was a Quinn listed.

Dot looked at me quizzically.

"Have you found something, dear?"

"I think I just hit paydirt, Dot." It turned out that Dot knew quite a bit about the Quinns of Huallan. It seemed there had only been one child, Hilary, who went off to the big city to become Somebody. Mr. Quinn suffered a stroke after being hailed out two seasons running, and Mrs. Quinn had moved to Edmonton to be near her daughter. Apparently, although she held onto the land for years, she finally sold the farm once she knew that Hilary would never marry and come home.

Dot had gone to school with Hilary, but she said she didn't know all that much about her. I figured if Dot didn't get to know everything about someone, there was something wrong. She already had enough on me to produce a reasonable genealogical chart, and I'd only met her yesterday. She'd grown up with Quinn, but now the fountain of information was starting to dry up.

I offered to put the kettle on for another pot of tea. Dot would have none of it, and began bustling around the kitchen like a banty hen. Never one to be overly pushy when it came to chores, I sat back.

"So she went off to the Big City and never looked back?"

Dot ran tap water into the kettle.

"I wouldn't say that, exactly, dear. Her mother was buried here, and she comes here every summer, after all. It's just that she never really socializes with any of us, and there's a lot of us still around and rather active."

From what I had seen of the county fair, this was an understatement. That wasn't the point that interested me, however.

"She comes up here every summer? But I thought her mother sold the farm."

"The farm yes, the cottage no. It was something else when they bought that property out on Trumpeter Lake. I mean can you imagine wanting to spend your holidays cooking on a stove even more rustic than the one you use all year long? What is so relaxing about chopping wood when you do that at home? It seems that Mrs. Quinn, she was from Ontario originally, had to have a "summer place" as she called it. I remember my mother and her set howling when they heard about it."

"So Dr. Quinn comes out to this summer cottage every year?"

"Hmmm. From what I hear, she's got it pretty well winterized by now. The Giebelhaus boy had the job of insulating it as I recall."

"So you see her up here quite often?"

"Not really. I mean we know they're here, but they just don't seem to want to connect with anybody. There have been rumours, that, well. . . " For the first time in the day, Dot looked rather uncomfortable wading through someone else's biography. "But I suppose they always say that about brainy ladies that don't get married; what with Gertrude Stein and all."

"People here think that Dr. Quinn is a lesbian?"

I should have trundled out a euphemism; Dot looked uncomfortable with the word hanging in the air. There was something else bothering me about what she'd just said, though, something that hadn't come up before.

It hit me just as the kettle started to sing.

"They?"

Chapter 17

It seemed like ages before Guy picked up the phone. The operator cut in over my answering "Hello."

"I have a collect call from a Randy Craig, will you accept the charges?"

"I suppose so," Guy drawled.

"Never try joking with paid officials, Guy, especially not when they have the power to cut me off."

"Hold on, ma'am, since when does someone instigating a collect call have the right to tell someone off without even saying hello?"

"I did say hello, and thanks for accepting the charges. There's no phone in my motel room, and I couldn't figure out the change system on this phone. I did wait till after six o'clock so the charges would be lower."

"Doesn't make much difference once you add on the collect charges. Whatever. Great to hear from you. Where are you and why are you calling me collect?"

It was great to hear Guy's voice. I told him all about the rumours I'd harvested from Dot Lewis. Guy whistled over the phone, nearly deafening me.

"And you think the "other woman" was Ahlers? How come you're so sure it's not her mother or sister or someone?"

"She doesn't have a sister. And her mother is dead. Anyhow, you should have heard the tone her voice took on when she started talking about 'how people like to talk.' Besides, while "far be it from Dot to spread a malicious rumour" this other woman seemed pretty young, or anyway as young as Quinn, when they'd catch sight of her."

"What do you mean, catch sight of her?"

"Well, it seems that she never came into town to do shopping, but the lake is pretty well overrun with pleasure boats during the summer, and people would spot two women around the place." A wind blew at the phone booth door, and I suddenly remembered the coast of our little conversation. "So anyway, I thought I'd just phone to let you know I'd be in Grande Prairie instead of Peace River for the next few days."

Guy's voice took on a note of suspicion.

"Randy? What are you planning on doing?"

"Well, I thought I might take a little tour out to Trumpeter Lake."

"Alone? You must be out of your mind. You can't go snooping around Quinn's cottage."

"Why not?"

"What if she's out there? What kind of an excuse would you have? I can see the headlines now, EX-GRAD STUDENT FOILED IN ATTEMPT TO MURDER PROF."

"Don't be so melodramatic, Guy." He wasn't even close to spooking me, but the wind whistled through the phone door again, and I shivered.

"Listen, Randy, where are you staying?"

"The Swan Motel. Why?"

"Why? Because I'm coming up there is why."

"Why? Don't you trust me?"

"In a word, no. Anyhow, there's nothing much happening down here right now anyway."

"How are you getting here?"

"I'll take the bus."

"It's a six-hour trip."

"That's okay, I care enough to send the very best. Just sit tight until I get there tomorrow."

I smiled in spite of myself.

"Randy?"

"Yes?"

"Scout around for a good pizza joint."

During the next fifteen hours I did some heavy soul searching and some light reading. I was wondering about why I'd phoned Guy with my discovery. I hated to admit it, but I think it had something to do with my discomfort with the lesbian connection of Dr. Quinn.

I've never considered myself particularly leery of homosexuality. I have a few gay friends, although I must admit they're all men and they're for the most part discreet. I can't help it; I've never thought sex was something one took along to Show and Tell. I thought I was liberal when it came to the third sex. Apparently not.

Dot Lewis had hit the nail on the head when she talked about academics and lesbianism in the same sentence. And that's what was bugging me. There has always been this sort of snide association between the two, as if women only applied their brains if men weren't on their minds. Maybe that's why I'd phoned Guy, to prove to myself that I could handle both at the same time.

On the other hand, maybe I was overanalyzing the whole situation. Maybe all I had needed was a friend to talk to. I decided to let Sherry Hite worry about that one, and proceeded to navigate the lumps in the mattress toward oblivion.

Waking up presented no problems. Birds were singing, Guy was on his way, and huge semis were roaring along the road outside my window. I showered and dressed, and went out to forage for breakfast.

Primitive man had it easy. I eschewed a Macdonald's in favour of a Phil's, thinking that pancakes and eggs would keep me going longer for the money. A waitress who had obviously modelled herself on the character in *Five Easy Pieces* snapped her gum as she took my order. Soon a plate of pancakes, sausages and eggs was slid in front of me, and the bill was slipped into the handy niche in the salt and pepper holder. I noticed she signed her name with a very round, childish, hand and dotted the "i" with a heart. I bet it did wonders for tips. I polished the cutlery with my paper napkin.

Guy was Greyhound grumpy for about an hour but cheered up after catching sight of his seventeenth swan. We tacitly refrained from discussing the next day's plans. Instead we ate an anchovy-free but otherwise laden pizza, caught a movie, and headed back for the motel.

I know that boxers and footballs players refrain the night before, but we weren't planning on battering anyone the next day, so what the hell.

Chapter 18

We'd driven down the road three times before I spotted
the two tire tracks meandering off the beaten path behind a
large copse of Balm of Gilead. Guy had started to protest as
I nosed the car toward them.

"What are you doing?"

"This has got to be it. The grocer said it was between the
Bide-a-while and the Dew Drop By and we've been back and
forth between them."

"But this isn't even a road; self-respecting goats would
turn up their noses at this!"

"I'm sure this is the road in."

"You did take out complete coverage on this car, didn't
you?"

"Guy!"

It seemed that "summer places" had caught on since old
Mrs. Quinn's day. Trumpeter Lake was surrounded by cabins.
Some of them had that all year look, but those on this side of
the lake were charmingly unkempt with silly names, like
proper cabins should be.

We made several sharp turns through the long grasses
and bushes and suddenly popped out into a clearing. The cabin
looked much like cabins should, just older than most. There
was a wooden porch leading to a screened door, a wooden door
behind the screen. Small windows looked over the parking
green. I presumed the picture window faced the lake beyond.
An outhouse painted the same rusty red as the cabin sat off

in the woods to the left. A lean-to shed next to the cabin seemed to house storm windows, a push mower and cobwebs.

There was no other car in sight, but I was nervous anyway. When you're persona non grata with someone, it doesn't do to drop in unannounced. Breaking and entering is another matter.

I hadn't discussed a gameplan with Guy, but he was beginning to sense where my mind was headed. He cleared his throat.

"Cat burglary isn't one of my fortes, you know."

"Who said anything about stealing cats?" I countered, with more breeziness than I honestly felt. "I just want to look around."

"Sure, isn't that what Hitler said about Poland?"

"Since when did you turn in your Amoral Anonymous membership card?"

Guy rose up in his seat, wounded.

"Just what is that supposed to mean?"

"Anyone who is so into games should have no problems with playing on the fringes of danger."

"I'll have you know that anyone with a love of games is a most moral person. To whom else are rules of such vital importance, I ask you?"

There was no way to win this one so I let it drop and put the car into Park. I turned the key off, and the birds went up in volume.

I felt as if I was trespassing as soon as I stepped out of the car. Well, I guess, technically, I was. I've never quite figured it out. If they don't put up a No Trespassing sign and then shoot you anyway, are they legally in the right?

Despite his compunctions, Guy followed me around to the lakeside of the cabin. I could see why old Mrs. Quinn put up with the teasing about her summer place. The view from the front porch was gorgeous.

There is something about the colour green in the Peace River Country that is unlike a green in any other place on earth. Maybe it's the combination of all the different greens put together, but whatever it is, it's enough to knock your eye teeth out every time you turn a corner and come up against it.

The grass was lighter than the leaves of the poplars which were lighter in turn than the Balm of Gilead which gave way to the darker pines. The lake reflected all these colours and added a bluey-green of its own to the spectrum.

The dock was unpainted; a wooden road leading to nowhere straight out from the cabin's back door. There was a small sandy beach, a lawn with an old picnic table, and a canoe drawn up and turned over next to the trees. A picture window took in the whole scene. It was this window that Guy was glueing himself to, shading his eyes to peer inside the cabin.

"What do you see?" I came up behind him.

"Not much. A fireplace, an overstuffed couch, some wicker chairs, a desk, and I think this thing over to the right here is the edge of the kitchen table."

He was close to being a compleat cataloguer. Two doors led off from the room he'd described, and the kitchen seemed to take up the corner to the right of the window. I rattled the door beside the window although I knew it would be useless; there was a newish looking Yale lock gleaming at me from shoulder height.

Guy, in the meantime, had headed around the far side of the cabin.

"Randy. Come here, I think I found what you're looking for."

I picked my way through the long grass and found him removing a screen from a high window. The butterfly bolts seemed disinclined to budge, but Guy soon had the screen leaning beside him. He then pulled out a Swiss Army knife and inserted it in the lock of the window. With one twist, the window was unlocked, and Guy was shoving it open.

I was impressed.

"Where did you learn to do that?"

"Oh, I've developed a plethora of skills over the years."

"What about all that hoohah about morality?"

"Really, Randy, morality is a choice one makes, not a blind compulsion. If one were not cognisant of the options, how could one make an informed choice?"

I shook my head at Guy's semantics.

"Oh forget it, it's a long story. Now are you going to climb in here, or do I stand around holding this sash up all day?"

Put that way, I could hardly refuse. I hooked one foot onto Guy's bent knee and hoisted myself up over the sill.

I've never been the most graceful of people, but I don't think there is a delicate way of entering a house by means of a window. I was stranded with my arms and upper torso dangling in forbidden territory and, for a second, I felt like giving up. It was the realization of what Guy's perspective must be on this scene that inspired a burst of scrambling which led to me doing an awkward somersault onto a bed about two and a half feet below the window.

I was in a dark little room, presumably behind one of the two doors we had seen. The only light was coming from the window. Guy's voice was coming from the same direction.

"Do you think you can find your way to the deck door, or do I have to follow your example of little cat feet?"

I groaned and slid off the chenille bedspread, making a mental note to straighten it before we left.

Motes of dust hung in the air of the main room. They probably were everywhere, but there was more light by which to see them in here. I headed for the deck. The Yale slid back and clicked open. Guy entered the room like Inspector Clousseau after Cato, but ruined the mood by sneezing several times in a row.

"There went the atmosphere," I shrugged.

"It's the so-called atmosphere that's making me sneeze," Guy rejoined after blowing his nose into an oversized hankie. "Doesn't the woman ever clean the place?"

"It's a summer cabin, Guy. Who knows when she was here last? All that grocer said was that she closed late last fall. That could mean anything from the day after Labour Day till Hallowe'en."

"All right. So what exactly do you expect to find here?"

"Evidence."

"Evidence of what? Slatternly housekeeping?"

It was hard to answer Guy's question so I sniffed and turned my back on him. I wasn't sure what I was looking for. I just had a feeling that I would know it when I found it. Guy began to open kitchen cupboards. Like a magnet, I made for the desk. Unlike the dusty cabin, this area was pin-in-place perfect. Pens and pencils were arranged in the top drawer. Letter and legal sized pads of bond paper were in the second. I found a couple of packages of carbon paper in the third drawer.

I used to use carbon paper all the time in the days before my trusty Kaypro came into my life. One always made a copy of everything, because you never knew when some well-meaning assistant was going to tidy the producer's desk and lose your masterpiece. I wondered why Dr. Quinn didn't just bring her PC up to the cabin with her. Then it occurred to me that I couldn't see any grounded sockets in the cabin, so maybe she just left high tech to her urban run.

Guy had continued from the kitchen through to the bedroom that I hadn't used as an access point.

"Randy, come here."

I entered a larger room than the other bedroom. There was an ironframe double bed covered with the requisite chenille spread and a large closet set into the wall. Side tables stood on either side of the bed.

Guy was standing in the open doorway of the closet.

"What is it?" I asked, trying to peer around the bulk of my fellow investigator.

"Evidence," said Guy drily, stepping back to allow me to see.

Chapter 19

The closet was divided the way I've always imagined the Red Sea parted, with hangers shoved to either side. On the left were assorted flowered tops and pedal pushers; standard cottage garb. On the right was a collection of very frilly feminine dresses.

I could understand what Guy meant. In a million years, neither of us could imagine Hilary Quinn in one of those frothy concoctions. It'd be like sticking a carrot into a Singapore Sling. They reminded me of what Carol Burnett used to wear as her character Eunice.

"They aren't hers."

"No."

"Maybe her mother's?"

"They couldn't be. I mean, I'm not sure when she died, but these dresses are current style, if you can use the word style to describe them."

"So they're someone else's."

"Yes."

"And they could be Ahlers', is that what you're thinking?"

"Well, why not, Guy?"

"Because it fits too neatly."

"What do you mean?"

"I mean that, if this were a mystery novel, then these would be Ahlers' and we'd discover that Quinn was her lover and murdered her in a fit of pique. But there's one problem. This is real life. Things like that don't happen."

"Joe Orton was killed in real life."

"That's close to being a perfect oxymoron, Randy. Anyhow, there's one other reason that they can't be Ahlers' clothes."

"What's that?"

"How could such a tasteful writer dress so tackily?"

I smiled inwardly at Guy's superficiality, but he did have a point. There was something a little too loud, a little too gaudy about those dresses. They screamed from the confines of the closet. Those dresses could make a statement three counties away. No wonder the grocer was so sure there'd been folks around the cottage. From his vantage point across the lake, he wouldn't have been able to miss these walking flower gardens.

While my eyes were glazing over staring at the printed frills, Guy continued to poke around. I shook myself and went after him. A storage closet contained an ironing board, brooms, an old dressmaker's dummy and the water heater. The small bedroom had no closet, just a chest of drawers and the small iron bed I'd met previously. I was glad Quinn hadn't put the dresser under the window. I straightened the bedspread, opened and closed the dresser drawers, and pulled down the window sash and relocked it.

By this time Guy was outside refastening the storm window. I closed the bedroom door behind me. Everything looked the way we had found it. I checked the big bedroom and was glad I had. I must have dropped the open packet of carbon paper on the bed in my surprise over Guy's discovery. I picked it up and pushed at the closet door even though it appeared to be well and truly closed.

"Randy, let's get out of here."

Guy sounded strained. I glanced around once more, shut the bedroom door and made my way to the deck door. Guy had tripped the lock and was waiting for me in the doorway. I stepped out into the freshest air I'd ever breathed. It felt as if I'd been holding my breath the whole time we'd been inside. Guy pulled the door closed and shook it to be sure before he turned back to me. His smile did a reverse Cheshire and disappeared from his face.

"What's that?" he asked.

"What's what?" I looked down to where he pointed, and my heart plummeted down to sit awhile with my appendix. "Oh my God." I stared at the carbon paper still in my hand. I looked around frantically. "I'll throw it away."

"And have someone wonder what's up if they find it? The object is to make it seem as if we have never been here, not broadcast the fact."

"Well, what should I do?" I wailed.

Guy looked pained.

"Oh, bring it with us and we'll ditch it somewhere. No one ever remembers how much carbon paper they have. She'll probably never miss it."

"There is another unopened packet in there," I volunteered.

"In that case, we're home free." Guy opened the passenger door and stepped back to let me in. I handed him the car keys and sank into the bucket seat clutching the only item I had ever stolen in my life. I was a burglar. I wondered if some cosmic Victor Hugo would sick a Javert on me for a half-empty packet of carbon paper. I had a feeling Quinn wouldn't like it one bit.

Chapter 20

I didn't notice much of the ride back. I was too immersed in the problems I seemed to have created on this trip. I had come up to discover a setting for Ahlers' life, and instead had stumbled on a reason for her death.

"Let's review things, okay?"

"Fine by me," said Guy with his eyes straight ahead.

"Ahlers seems to have been writing about the Peace River Country."

"Check."

"Quinn comes from and still maintains a cottage in the Peace River Country."

"Check."

"No one knows Ahlers but they all know about Professor Quinn and her ladyfriend."

"Check."

"And Quinn, the stolid professor, seems to have some sort of in with Ahlers."

"What do you mean?"

"Well, she has scooped everyone with an article after each novel comes out. It's as if she's the first person to read them."

"So?"

"Well, maybe she is the first person to read them."

Guy snorted.

"Why would a world class writer hand over her manuscripts to a by-and-large unknown English professor? Pretty pricey proofreader, maybe?"

I refused to rise to Guy's ribbing.

"All I'm saying is that Hilary Quinn and Margaret Ahlers are close."

"Ah, the Dot Lewis lesbian theory?"

"What does it matter? Close enough to be intimate about their work. I think Ahlers let her best friend read her novels first just to give her a break in the academic business. Why are you slowing down?"

"I thought I'd pull in here so we could stretch our legs."

I looked at the campground sign. It said "Waskahigan River Campsite." I checked the map to see where we were. The only campsite on this side of the road was marked "House River." I asked Guy about it.

"It's a very old map?" he offered.

"Or that's a very new sign," I countered.

After he'd pulled up by a picnic table, he took a look at the map.

"Same place, as far as I can tell."

"Well, what do you think Waskahigan means?"

"Probably means "house"."

I snorted, and went off to the little waskahigan marked "ladies." When I got back, Guy was alternating touching his toes and stretching his arms over his head.

It looked like a good idea, but I've never been much on joining in on good ideas. I prefer to come up with them. Instead of exercise, I set myself to cleaning out the junk from the floor of the car. It's amazing how quickly juice boxes and gum wrappers can multiply. I took one handful to the garbage bin and headed back to shake out the floor mats.

As I was pulling out my floor mat, the fateful packet of carbon paper came with it. I'd shoved it under my seat and forgotten my shame. Now it surfaced again like my own peculiar albatross. Well, the only thing to do was to get rid of it. I pulled it out forcefully and sheets of flimsy blue paper escaped, flying everywhere.

"Shit." This exclamation got through to Charles Atlas, and, laughing, he began to chase carbon paper like an actress chasing butterflies in a tampon commercial. I was scrabbling at the ones nearest me when something brought me up short.

Most of the packet had never been used, but someone had shoved a little-used piece of carbon back into the plastic. On it was centered the words:

Feathers of Treasure a novel by Margaret Ahlers.

I screamed. Guy paused in his Catherine Deneuve dirvish.

"What's the matter? Did you see a snake?"

I was so excited I hardly registered the semi-chauvinistic tone. Guy's consciousness could get raised later.

"What do you think of this?" I shouted, waving the incriminating carbon in Guy's face.

"I think it's carbon paper," he said.

"No, no, look what's cut into it."

He squinted at the paper and then whistled slowly.

"It looks like you may be right after all."

"Of course I am, as if there was any doubt," I chirped, but deep down, I was not sure whether or not I was glad or terrified that I'd been vindicated. After all, it's one thing to suspect that someone has murdered someone, but quite another thing to have it proved.

It was as if Guy was reading my mind.

"It's not exactly irrefutable proof, you know."

"What do you mean?"

"Just because you found that in Quinn's cabin doesn't mean she killed Ahlers. God, it doesn't even mean she knew Ahlers -- she could have just been jacking around on the typewriter."

"With carbon paper? That's like doodling in oil paint."

"You know what I mean."

"No I don't. First of all, this means that it's very likely there is a fourth novel, for all Quinn's hot air. For another thing, it makes a direct link between Quinn and Ahlers. For another thing, it connects the reports of two women, and the two different wardrobes in the cabin. I think it's incredibly significant."

"Okay, so it's incredibly significant. What are you going to do about it?"

I stopped and stared at him. There was a moment or two of pugnacious silence before we began to laugh. It really was a silly scene; Guy was glowering and I was trying to stare him down, clutching a dirty piece of carbon paper. It's lucky we were the only ones in the campsite. People'd have been burning their marshmallows right left and centre, watching us.

"I haven't the faintest idea. What do you think I should do with it?"

"The logical reply would be that you should go home, write your thesis, and forget all about this."

"We may be talking about murder, though."

"We may be talking fantasy. You really have no justification in assuming that Ahlers was murdered. If that's the case, we're almost certainly talking slander."

"You really are hung up on these rules, aren't you?"

"Well, if you don't need my advice, what do you intend to do about it? Go to the police and say you've discovered a murder on the grounds that you broke into a summer cabin and stole some carbon paper?"

My elation crumbled. Of course I had no proof. All I had was my theory that Ahlers was describing the Peace Country in her novels and a crumpled piece of carbon paper with an odd new title on it. I was beginning to feel very silly. I sat down on the picnic bench and scuffed my shoe in the gravel. I felt all of seven years old.

Guy sat down next to me and draped a long warm arm over my shoulders.

"Don't take it so hard. I'll bet Sam Spade had his off days too."

"But Guy, it was all making so much sense."

"Exactly why you should stop and question it. Nothing should make that much sense in this day and age. We are living in the world of open texts, after all."

"Oh, give me a break." The last thing I needed was a lecture on postmodernist theory. What I did need was a bath. The blue from the carbon paper was all over my hands. I looked around, but the only source of water other than the river seemed to be the hand pump. I opted for the river.

When I came back up the bank, wiping my hands on the backs of my jeans, Guy was already sitting in the car. On the passenger side.

The next four hours were taken up with white knuckle driving. I kept flashing onto the scenes of the truck driver hauling a semi full of toilets in Abbey's *The Brave Cowboy.* My fellow drivers, most of them in semis, took the speed limit signs as suggested minimums. I wondered how many of them were wired on caffeine and uppers. When I finally hit the Yellowhead's divided stretch I felt like I'd been given a reprieve from death row. We'd all but ceased conversation by this time, so Guy's voice startled me a little.

"Supposing there was a fourth novel. Where do you think it is now?"

Chapter 21

It seemed like the next few days after our trip to the Peace River Country blurred into stills with weeping sepia edges. Nothing seemed to connect and nothing seemed to get done either. I was in a fog, wandering from my apartment to the department and back again. Every now and then I'd punctuate my time with a coffee at Java Jive with Maureen or whoever else was headed that way.

Summers on campus are a strange thing. There's a distant bustle of spring and summer session students, but the upper office floors could be used as bowling alleys most of the time, they're that empty. A lot of professors go off to conferences or to visit distant special collections or, heaven forbid, go on holiday. Most grad students start taking things a little bit easier than they have done in winter session. In fact, by the middle of June the Rasputin-on-a-bad-day look has faded from most everyone's eyes. For all I knew, it had even faded from mine.

I wasn't seeing too much of Guy since the trip. I wasn't sure, but I felt a coolness that hadn't been present before the long car ride home. Since the weather had gotten nice, I wasn't staying inside all that much when I was home, and the library had better air circulation than my office, so who knows, maybe he'd been phoning me without getting through. I didn't really care. I was feeling too preoccupied to be worrying about our relationship, if you could call it that, and the sight of him reminded me of breaking into Quinn's cabin -- an incident I wasn't too proud of. At the same time I was trying to put Guy out of mind, I was still pondering what he'd said to me about the fourth manuscript.

Suppose there was a fourth novel somewhere. Where would it be? Had Ahlers left a will? Was there any way of finding out? It occurred to me that Garth, my publisher, might know about the laws of wills and especially willing copyrights and manuscripts. I was just about to pick up the phone and call him when another publisher's name leapt to mind. If anyone would know anything about Margaret Ahlers' effects, it would be her publishers, McKendricks.

A male voice answered the phone. I tried the truth on them this time; I was a graduate student working on Margaret Ahlers and could they tell me please where her papers were?

I made a mental note to try the truth more often; I was connected straight through to Duncan McKendrick. From what I remembered of the "Tarahna" literary scene, Duncan was the son and heir apparent to Daddy's empire. I couldn't quite figure out how old he was, probably in his mid-forties. I'm lousy with ages, anyway. I group people into three camps: under fifteen, over seventy, and in-between. Duncan was in the "older than me, younger than Mom" in-between category. I'd had him pointed out at a couple of wingdings, but I'm sure he had no idea who I was. That was okay with me. I figured I might get farther on the innocent student ploy.

"How may I help you, Ms. Craig?"

I launched into my grad student dilemma. I could almost hear him nodding sagely over the phone.

"I see. Of course you would want to examine Ahlers' papers for your study. Well, the only problem I have is that we're not free to divulge any information concerning the placement of the papers until it's been officially announced, and that won't be for, let me see, several months."

I had been puffing up expectantly throughout his little speech, but now I sagged. Months? My silence must have been loaded, because Duncan leapt into the breach with an inspired suggestion.

"Why don't you write your request, care of us here at McKendricks, and we'll see that it's passed on to the executor?

After all, I can't see that anyone would want to deliberately stymie an academic interest in Ms. Ahlers."

It was grasping at straws, but I thanked him and hung up the phone. What did I have to lose? I drafted a quick letter asking to be given an opportunity to examine the papers and went down to the department office to get an envelope. After opening several empty drawers that had once held envelopes by the gross, I finally asked one of the secretaries where they were being kept.

"Under lock and key. Part of the new budget cuts. Sorry!"

I trudged down the mall to buy a package of envelopes, feeling hard done by. The business envelopes were out of stock. I bought a package of ten designer colours and mailed off my letter to McKendricks in a neon fuscia special. I hoped that old Duncan had a pair of sunglasses handy.

Chapter 22

The character business came to me at about eleven on a hot June night. I was sitting at the kitchen table drinking iced tea and watching a spindly legged bug dart around the standing lamp in the corner. It was too humid to move, let alone kill anything. I was idly thinking about redecorating, which in my case meant moving tacky furniture from one dim corner to another. I wondered if the landlord would contribute toward wallpaper, and checked the walls to see which one I should attack.

The bulletin board with the big map of the province was still staring down at me from the opposite wall. I'd have to do something about that. If I took down the map, the cork would be too dark for the room. Maybe I could spraypaint the cork; I was getting sick of staring at Big Sky Country.

A slight breeze riffled the curtains and gave me the impetus to heave myself out of the chair for more iced tea. On the way to the fridge I yanked the pins out of the map. A bunch of file cards came tumbling down with it. As I bent down to pick them up, it occurred to me that the system I'd created on this wall had been what had sent me to the Peace River Country in the first place. I started to remove all the cards. It was ridiculous to even contemplate throwing them away (I have trouble pitching egg cartons), but I wasn't quite sure of what order to put them in.

Should I order them by location, or by which novel they came from, or alphabetically by the first word in the quotation? Idly, I began to cut and shuffle the cards. I finally decided to order them by novel. I'd written the title at the bottom of most of the quotations, but on some I'd just jotted page numbers.

It became a game. Would I be able to recognize the novel from a cryptic, area-specific quotation? I was doing pretty well until I came to the part where Andrea is picking saskatoons and becomes disoriented in the bush. For the life of me I couldn't remember whether that was from an early childhood sequence in *One for Sorrow* or one of the flashbacks in *The Children of Magpie*. It was driving me crazy, so even in that heat, I plodded into the living room to pull out my copies of the novels. Pouring myself some more iced tea, I began leafing through the third novel. Even before I hit page 83 I realized my mistake. The passage had to come from *One for Sorrow*, because the heroine in *The Children of Magpie* was Isabel, not Andrea.

I checked through the first novel, now dog-eared and pencilled throughout the margins, just to make sure. I was right. It came from the part where Andrea has gone to the farm for the summer and her grandmother has sent her out for saskatoons with two honey pails strapped to her waist. She dodges a hornet and trips, spilling saskatoons everywhere. After a good cry, she looks up and realizes that she's lost all sense of direction there on the ground among the bushes. For the first time in the farm context, she is pacified rather than frightened by the experience. She limps home eventually with next to nothing in the pails and purple stains all over her matching shorts and pop top.

It was a great sequence, and it finally occurred to me why I had mixed it up with the third novel. In The Children of Magpie, Isabel travels back home for her grandmother's funeral, and keeps travelling back in time to flashbacks similar to the saskatoon scene. There's the day her grandmother pushes the lawn chairs together and throws a quilt over them to make a playhouse for Isabel, and the time Isabel tries to be a home help for her grandmother when the old lady's laid up with arthritis. No wonder I'd mixed up the quotation. I closed the book, and returned to staring at the now empty cork wall.

Andrea and Isabel. They were the same woman. And, of the two characters in *Two for Joy*, Eleanor was far closer to the mold than her friend Marie. Andrea. Eleanor. Isabel. A. E. I. Why hadn't I seen it before?

The answer was simple. I'd been looking for locations before, stuff for my thesis. Now I was looking for Ahlers herself, any clue that could bring this author to life for me, now that it was too late. I don't know if I was already thinking of myself as some sort of literary Mrs. Peel at this point, but my urge to get Quinn for what ever she might have done to Ahlers had been percolating ever since I'd connected them in Dot Lewis' living room.

I know that authors are never completely autobiographical, and that most of the characters they create are amalgams of various people they have met, observed and imagined. I wasn't going to let that stop me, though. There was a throughline in these novels, and I was going to pinpoint it. In the same way that I'd let the novels lead me to the Peace River Country, I was going to let them lead me to their author. Maybe knowing how she'd lived would tell me how she'd died.

I decided I'd use pink cards for physical descriptions, green cards for thoughts and dreams, yellow cards for activities and events that might leave a mental or physical mark on the character. Starting tomorrow, the cork board would have a purpose once more. I put my glass and the empty pitcher in the sink, straightened the pile of novels and cue cards, and, for good measure, just before I turned out the light I swatted the bug. I was back on track.

Chapter 23

Will Rogers once said that being on the right track was fine and dandy, but you could still get run over by the train if all you did was sit around. I wasn't intending to sit around. I began preparing the next morning. I washed the floor, cleaned the apartment till everything was either gleaming or a reasonable facsimile thereof, dragged my folding grocery cart out of the storage closet and lugged home provisions from the Safeway. I also picked up packets of cue cards, pins, three new pens and two jumbo bags of strawberry licorice from the Shoppers Drug Mart next door. I figured I was in for a long haul.

It took most of the day to do all the chores I'd set for myself. Some people might find it ridiculous, but I'd discovered through experience that I had to get everything out of the way before beginning a project. If things got rough, defrosting the fridge might look inviting, and a trip to the store could be extended with ease to fill an entire afternoon. I had to get rid of externals before I could put my head down and concentrate.

I switched my telephone bell to mute, and left my machine to field calls. These days all I expected were calls offering to clean my non-existent carpets, but even telephone surveys had been known to distract me in the past. This was vital research and I wasn't going to take any chances on being sidetracked answering questions about instant coffee.

I had decided to start at the beginning and reread all three novels with my pen in hand. I figured that since this was at least my fourth time through each one, I should be able to spot character delineation without missing anything.

It was harder going than I'd thought it would be. The narrative kept winding around me, making me forget what it was I was looking for. I found that I'd have to back up constantly to find references my eyes had swept by. Aside from anything else, I could testify that Ahlers had been a spellbinding storyteller.

One for Sorrow reminded me of a quirky Alice Munro with a dash of Iris Murdoch thrown in to keep things jumping. Andrea, the main character whom I was betting was Ahlers herself, starts out as a child of eleven and ages about fifteen years through the novel. Each section focusses on an annual event: summer vacation, birthday, Thanksgiving, Christmas, Easter, first day of school, university exam week, convocation, Valentine's Day. The context told you how old she was in each situation, and they were roughly chronological. Explaining it makes it sound complicated, but it follows pretty naturally when you're reading it.

I was getting a feel for Andrea the physical person, but the original essence that I'd felt even on first reading the book was overpowering. It was as if, no matter what happened to her directly, like falling in the saskatoons or meeting the trick motorcycle carnie at the exhibition, she was always watching more than participating. Her glasses, which were constantly described because the frames seemed to change each section, seemed to act as portholes or proscenium arches or TV sets on the world. Andrea just wandered around behind them, not particularly selective with the channel switch.

I knew I was reading far more into the character than I could justify with page references, but at this stage that was fine with me. If I could get the groundwork done on Andrea, actualities and gut feelings together would give me a sense of how Eleanor and Isabel fit into the picture.

I finished *One for Sorrow* just before midnight. It had taken longer than usual with all the stops and starts for jotting things down. I looked up. The kitchen table was littered with cue cards of various colours. I grinned with self-satisfaction. I'd start pinning them up in the morning.

Sitting in one position had taken its toll on my back. It was as if I had to go through a refresher course in the history of evolution just to stand up. I had a shower and went to bed. I thought I'd dream of Andrea and her antics all night, but the gods smiled and I woke up fresh with no recollection of rapid eye movement whatsoever.

I spent the first hour after breakfast futzing around organizing my cue cards on the wall. I've never been a morning person; I have to edge into a day sideways. I start cooking around eleven and usually run out of steam around three. I figured that if I got all the chores out of the way quickly, I could get through *Two for Joy* by about two-thirty.

It was obvious that Eleanor was an extension of Andrea. Even the glasses figured again from time to time. It took me till chapter fifteen before I understood why I hadn't picked up on it before. Eleanor wasn't the heroine. Marie was front and center as soon as she came into the picture.

For those of you who haven't yet read *Two for Joy*, it focusses on the friendship-cum-rivalry of two women who have known each other for years. It's written in limited omniscient, from the point of view of society watching the two of them. Every now and then you come across a bit in italics written from the point of view of one of the women. For the longest time you think the voice is that of Eleanor, the retiring one who seems to follow everything that Marie does. After awhile, and I'm still not sure how she manages it, Ahlers makes the focus shift and you find yourself hitting your forehead with that classic "I-could-have-had-a-V8" action and shouting out loud "It's Marie!" All the time that the reader is sure that Marie is the creator and Eleanor the follower, Marie is actually milking Eleanor for ideas and then making a splash with them herself. She has fooled Eleanor, she has fooled the world, and she has almost fooled herself into thinking she's the innovator.

Once the reader cottons on to the fact that Marie is actually using Eleanor and sapping her of all her strength, you'd expect the book to go for the jugular. There Ahlers goes and fools you again. The book becomes almost lyrical in its treatment of Marie after this point. The fact that Eleanor allows Marie to use her seems to condemn her in the eyes of the reader, and even Marie herself is convinced by the end of the narrative that she is only doing what she has been doing because she has been forced to by means of Eleanor's passivity.

It's a complicated little plot at the best of times, and what with having to remember to juggle the italics back to Marie instead of identifying them with Eleanor, it took some time to get through it. I'd almost gauged it correctly, though. At three-thirty I looked up from the novel to find I'd managed to cover about fifty cue cards with notes and page references.

About half of them corresponded exactly with references from the first novel. The rest were what you'd expect to find of Andrea grown up a bit. I estimated the ages of Eleanor and Marie to fall in the 20-35 camp as the novel progressed.

I'd had to create a new category along the way. I turned the pink cards over to the unlined side and wrote things that other characters (in this case, mainly Marie) said about Eleanor. The authorial voice wove in and out of the narrative so much, it was difficult to distinguish it from that of Marie.

I had figured that *The Children of Magpie* would be the easiest of the three to go through for various reasons. For one thing, Isabel is front and center as the main character, and not only do we get her in the present at about thirty-five, we also get her flashbacked all over the place as a child and younger woman. I jumped right in after scoffing down some Kraft Dinner, figuring that I'd have at least half the book covered by the time my eyes gave out for the night.

As usual, I'd figured wrong. By eight-thirty I had only managed to get eleven cue cards filled, and I was getting bogged down. I put the book down and tried to figure out where I was going wrong.

I knew it wasn't the character: Isabel was obviously the extension of Andrea and Eleanor. She was quiet and very internalized. Unfortunately, for my purposes, there was not enough time spent on Isabel. She acted more as a lens for the action. Any information I did get was mainly old Andrea-covered territory. *Magpie*, which had practically led me like a Baedeker up to the Peace River Country, was not taking me anywhere close to Isabel. In fact, if there was anyone I got to know well, it was Isabel's grandmother.

Sure, there'd been a lot of focus on her in the first novel, but that was from the viewpoint of a child. The grandmother in *Magpie* was seen in hindsight, which they say is 20/20. I'm not so sure about that, and anyway it was buying into the old fallacy, making judgements about what a character written by a specific author does or doesn't remember about another character on two different occasions.

To make a long story shorter, I didn't find any glaring character discrepencies in my cue card reportage culled from the third novel. They obviously formed a loosely-knit trilogy; looser than say, the Lynne Reid Banks series on the single mother who sets up the antique shop or whatever it is, but on the same sort of track.

One for Sorrow, Two for Joy; if only there were a "three" in the third title. I looked at the titles I'd been doodling on a yellow cue card. Together, they looked like some sort of nursery rhyme, but not one I'd ever heard of. And why "Magpie", anyway? There was no reference to it in the novel, and I'd not come across any magpie references up in the Peace Country. Now, if only it had been a Trumpeter Swan, we'd have been cooking! Was it some Indian legend? I was going to have to hit the reference library tomorrow, I thought, which bothered me. Maybe I wasn't on the right track after all.

Chapter 24

I love libraries, especially the open stack variety. I've never managed to get my mind around the Library of Congress subject system, so unless I know the name or author of a particular book, I'm a lot better off combing the shelves once I've found the general area. Closed stacks are sort of like those fishing games at the county fair, you cast your hook, but you never know what you're going to get, or what's right next to it, that you should have asked for.

I tried Nursery Rhymes with no luck. Four and twenty blackbirds was as close as I could get to magpies there. I next tried bird books, from Audubon to local editions. Still no luck, but I learned that the magpie is a scrappy, thieving old bird that has taken to city life like helzapoppin. It was also apparently a nickname for an Anglican bishop. I had a feeling this wasn't what I wanted to know. Indian legends got me no further. The Micmacs have a legend about some geese and a turtle, and the coastal Indians favour the Sunbird and the Thunderbird, but as far as I could figure, neither of these feathered deities was a magpie.

After a discouraging morning I wended my way to the reference table. Knowing that I should have headed there first, I was also armed with the self-righteous knowledge that I had done my level best not to bother them. Seriously, my advice to anyone that wants to know something, and doesn't have all the time in the world to learn a lot of other stuff along the way, is to head right for the reference librarian or

archivist's desk. Not only do these people know how their
information storage systems work, they are also mines of
information in their own rights. I'd met a man in Kingston
once who was an expert on the history and craft of taxidermy,
and there's a woman at the Glenbow that knows the words to
all the old Wobbly strike tunes.

I wasn't expecting miracles this time, but I sure wasn't
going to leave an unturned stone in my wake either. The lady
smiled as I approached. The library can be a lonely place in
the summertime. She seemed to me to be about fifty, and when
she said hello she gave away her origin as somewhere in
England. I can't pinpoint regional dialects, but I felt safe
enough in guessing she was from the southern part of the
island. I smiled what I hoped was my winningest smile and
began what I knew was going to sound like a very strange
request.

"Magpies? You mean the black and white birds that you
see all over campus?"

"Yes, those are the ones. I was wondering if you knew
of any legends or local stories attached to them, or where I
might find such stories."

"My goodness, I'm not sure if I know of any. Wait a
moment, they're the birds my Auntie Jean used to count on,
aren't they!"

"I beg your pardon?"

"She'd spot them in groups and count them with a rhyme.
Now, what was it?"

The reference lady's brow was furrowing. While it was
a long shot, I figured I'd give it a try.

"It wouldn't go something like, 'One for sorrow, two
for. . . '"

"That's it!"she exclaimed. The desk librarians shot a
glance our way. Her voice modulated down quickly in
embarrassment, but her words hung in the air for me anyway.

"That's her rhyme:
'One for sorrow, two for joy,
Three for a girl, four for a boy,
Five for silver, Six for gold,

Seven for a story never told.'
I suppose it's odd to see seven together. It's a little fortune telling game, you see? Silly, I suppose. Now where else might there be something?"

She turned to her computer to see if she could locate anything else about the squawky birds, but I thanked her and made it out of the library in a semi-daze. I needed a cup of coffee. I'd have settled for a beer, but it was ten in the morning.

One for sorrow, two for joy. Three and four became the children of the magpie. I knew that there had to be a fourth novel. This wasn't a trilogy, it was a quartet. Somewhere, somehow, I was going to find a copy of Feathers of Treasure. Silver and gold.

Chapter 25

It was about ten-thirty and I'd been pacing around my apartment all night. I felt like a computer cursor buffeting through a program on sensory overload. I was almost literally bouncing off the walls trying to figure out what to do next. It was really no wonder I almost had a heart attack when I spotted the face at the window.

Being as far north as it is, Edmonton boasts long, light summer nights. Even so, at ten-thirty on the twenty-eighth of June there is enough shadow cast about to make even your mother look like the Garneau Grabber. I screamed.

The face didn't run away. I screamed again and began pawing for the phone which was somewhere on the wall beside me. I had the receiver in my hand before I realized that the face belonged to Guy. With my heart still doing areobics, I made my way up the stairs to let him in.

"You scared me half to death," I sputtered at him, but he was too busy chewing me out to hear me. I was crazy, I was impossible to reach, I put people into the awkward position of worrying about me, why hadn't I answered my phone messages, now I was overreacting and making him feel like a Peeping Tom. I had a feeling that blame for the greenhouse effect was going to be laid at my door at any minute -- something to do with the deodorant I used, probably. I am always amazed at peoples' capacity to designate blame. There was really nothing to do but let Guy run his course. I turned my back on him and plugged in the kettle.

I had mugs and milk out on the table and the water was almost boiling when he finally stopped for breath. Because I knew it would really bug him, I apologized. It had been careless of me to disregard my phone machine, but the truth was I'd forgotten about it. I'd got the machine because people were always chewing me out for not being available when they wanted me. Now I was getting chewed out anyway. Life was not fair.

My meek reply deflated Guy's pomp like nobody's business. I grinned as he sat down and accepted a cup of tea. Even with the tongue-lashing, I was really glad to see him. I was longing to tell him about the magpie verse, and the character connection, but something warned me to keep my trap shut. After all, he had been pretty distant recently. Besides, I was curious to know what had brought him here. I couldn't put a date on the last time I'd seen him. Maybe my mother did have cause to worry about my marital future.

"So do I have to go rewind my phone machine, or are you going to tell me what you want?"

Guy looked smug.

"Do not ask what you can do for your fellow grad student. Ask what your fellow grad student can do for you."

"You came over in the middle of the night, scaring me half to death, to do me a favour? I think it's time you looked up your Emily Post, my boy."

"You neglect to realize that had you, as a reasonable human being, deigned to notice your phone machine, I would not have had to stoop to the ignominy of tapping on your basement window."

"That's as that may be, but you still haven't told me what you want."

"Let me savor the moment; it's not often that I'm in a position to be magnanimous."

"Maybe I will go listen to that phone machine."

"It's full of cryptic but urgent messages. This is not the sort of thing you spout over the phone line."

"Guy! Will you tell me already?"

"Okay. As you may have noticed, I've been spending a wee bit of time with my third reader lately."

"Your third reader?"

"Hilary Quinn." He read the puzzlement on my face. "Oh, I assumed you knew. She has no position even remotely close to my thesis, but for some reason it was politic at the time to ask her."

"Hilary Quinn is your third reader."

"There's an echo in here, Randy. You should have that seen to." He crossed his long hairy legs, making himself more comfortable. He really had very nice legs, especially in shorts; a soccer player's legs. "Are you listening?"

"Of course I'm listening. You've been consorting with the enemy."

"I had a feeling you might take it this way. Let me explain. Think of me not as a traitor so much as an infiltrator. Kind of a Trojan Horse, if you receive my meaning."

Guy went on to explain that he had talked the Ice Lady into lending him her office for the rest of the summer while she was off "doing research." The upshot was that he had access to Quinn's office, and he was offering me a wallow in forbidden mud. Would I like to see the interior of some fascinating filing cabinets?

Would I.

Chapter 18

To say I was too excited to get much sleep that night could be a winning entry in the Guinness Book of Records as Understatement of the Year. I could almost taste victory. In less than twenty-four hours I was sure I was going to lay eyes on Ahlers' fourth novel.

I wasn't sure what kept me from telling Guy about my discoveries. Maybe it was my suspicions of Guy. I tried to shake the feeling; after all, he was doing me an incredible favour, but all the same I was uneasy. How loyal should one be to one's third reader? I didn't know; M.A candidates don't usually know their third readers, they come from another department on campus. Ph.Ds were a whole new ball of string.

Could Guy have been tagging along this whole time on Quinn's orders? Was there really something sinister going on or was this all my imagination? How could Guy wangle Quinn's office from her without being close? That was no mystery; I'd seen Guy work his charms on all and sundry, provided they were female. On the other hand, wasn't Quinn supposed to be gay? Would Guy's charms work on her at all?

I decided, or rather, my body decided to give the puzzle a rest at about four in the morning. I'd set my alarm for seven and woke bleary-eyed to a rainy day. Half of me was rejoicing; the rain would cool down my basement suite. The other half was wondering how on earth I was going to sneak into Quinn's office wearing my bright yellow sou'wester.

I needn't have worried. Guy met me at Java Jive and bought me a seventy-five cent cup of heaven. He told me that

Quinn's nearest office neighbour was off on naval exercises and that he hadn't spotted anyone else in the hallway all morning. Quinn's office was in the far north-east corner of the fourth floor. All I had to do was go up the far stairwell to the fourth floor and duck into the office. None of the English eyes who would know I shouldn't be there would be there to see me, and the Religious Studies folk across the hall wouldn't know me from Adam. I pointed out to Guy that this was an unfortunate choice of words, and that the Religious Studies folk would probably know Adam if they spotted him. Guy gave only a nod for what I thought was quite witty under the circumstances. I couldn't believe how nervous I was.

Guy was right about the ease of access to Quinn's lair. No one saw me go in, I was sure of it.

"You've got one day, and be neat about it. If you have to go out for any reason, unlock the door and close it behind you."

"Aren't you staying?"

"No. One felony per term is enough for me. Besides, I have a dissertation to write."

"Where are you going?"

"I'll be in the library most of the day. I'll phone you later, shall I?"

All of a sudden I was nervous again.

"Yes, call me tonight, after ten. If I don't answer, come find me."

Guy must have seen the sudden panic across my face.

"Hey, don't worry it. What can happen to you in the Humanities Building?"

"Right," I laughed, a little shakily. "I'll talk to you later."

"Right," he said and gave me a swift kiss. "Good luck, Randy. I hope this is what you really want." He strode down the hallway leaving me to curse his cryptic soul. Just what had he meant by that?

I closed the door and leaned back against it, surveying the uncharted landscape I was about to dive into. My mouth felt dry and my hands felt sweaty. I reached out for the drawer pull of the filing cabinet nearest to me.

Three hours later I was no longer nervous, just tired and dusty. I had been through every drawer and file in Quinn's territory, and there was nothing on Ahlers except for a few files of rough drafts of Quinn's previously published articles on the novels. I plonked myself down in Quinn's swivel chair and began to turn myself around aimlessly. There had to be a clue to the fourth novel here somewhere.

The only other pieces of furniture in the office besides the desk and computer table were the bookcases. Bookcases lined the walls and ran underneath the windows. Maybe the manuscript was in a hollowed out book. I tried to recall where that useless piece of detective trivia had come from, but at that point it seemed worth a try. I decided to flip through all books over an inch thick. I was going to go for books that were larger than 8 1/2 x 11 inches, and then I remembered the photocopy reducer in the main office, and decided that any size book was fair game.

I was halfway around the room when I struck paydirt. I was lugging a hardback Norton-like anthology off the shelf. The size looked promising. *Literature: Art and Artifice* must have been a good four inches thick. I pitied anyone who might be stuck with it assigned as primary reading. Lugging this around could give Arnold Schwarzenegger a hernia.

I tried riffling from back to front, but it was no go. The pages seemed to be stuck together. My heart began to beat faster. I sat the book on the desk and opened it to the first page. As I leafed past the frontispiece and the table of contents I got more and more excited. As my excitement built, I slowed down my actions to accentuate the anticipation. I just knew that in a page or two I would be looking at Feathers of Treasure, Ahlers' final novel.

I was wrong. What I found in the book safe, for that indeed is what it was, was four floppy disks. All they had for identification was a number in the left upper corner: 1, 2, 3, and 4. Was this what I was looking for? Why would Quinn input an entire manuscript onto floppy disks? Where were the two copies of Ahlers' last novel? (I knew there had to be two copies, otherwise why bother with carbon paper?) Inputting a whole novel? That was one humungous load of typing. Well, it was the only lead I had. I turned my attention to Quinn's computer. I just hoped she hadn't taken her command disk with her.

I found her command diskettes in the left drawer of her desk. Thank God, I thought, she uses Wordstar. The last thing I needed was to figure out another computer language in twenty minutes.

My happiness was short lived. Quinn may have guilelessly relinquished her office keys to Guy's big green eyes, but she locked her computer work with passwords.

Second guessing an enemy can sometimes be easier than second guessing a friend. Having to second guess anyone is a pain in the ass.

I had worked my way through all the characters' names in Ahlers' opus and most of the place names after about two hours of steady plodding. On the theory that the vowels would fall in order, I tried every girl's name that I could think of that began with an O. I tried all forms of the magpie nursery rhyme that I could think of. My eyes were begining to blur from staring at the green blinking of the screen. I leant back in the chair and tried to right my tired eyes by focussing on alternating far and middle distances. I stared out at the High Level Bridge. I moved my head slightly to the right and stared at the McNaught painting of the lake with the mega-horizons.

I hadn't looked at the painting closely since I entered the office, but now I couldn't seem to take my eyes off it. When I'd first seen it I'd been captivated by the stylishness of the work. Armed now as I was with first hand knowledge of the Peace Country, I recognized the realism behind the abstract lines. That was Trumpeter Lake, I'd stake my life on it. It was almost exactly the same view as I had seen out of Quinn's cabin.

A devilishly simple idea stole through my brain. The floppies had been found in a book subtitled Art and Artifice. Obviously, things were not what they seemed. Well, two could play at that game. I wasn't looking for an Ahlers name, I was looking for a Quinn name. I turned to the computer keyboard and typed in EUPHEMIA.

For a moment, nothing happened. Then the screen went temporarily blank. I was beginning to think I'd broken Quinn's computer when the cursor began to move across the screen. Trailing in its wake, like a banner behind a biplane, were the words Feathers of Treasure: A Novel by Margaret Ahlers.

I checked the length of the files on the disk. The novel ran about 350K. As much as I wanted to read it right away, I knew that the best idea was to get a copy. It would be an easy matter to copy it all onto another diskette, but it wouldn't do me much good once I was out of Quinn's office. I'd have to get a hard copy. I glanced at Quinn's old-style printer. Why didn't they equip profs with laser printers, or even bubble jets? This was going to take forever.

I checked the printer ribbon and paper supply, and then set the On switch alight. The PRINT program was a one command affair, and pretty soon the office was echoing with the most irritating sounds known to modern man. Pages were churning out about seven a minute. I calculated that I was in for about seven hours of cacophony. I thanked the powers that govern inspiration for reminding me to throw a set of foam ear plugs in my purse, and settled into Quinn's easy chair with her copy of *Daisy Circus*. As much as I wanted to read Ahlers' novel, I wasn't about to read line by line out of the printer. That kind of behavior was enough to drive you mad in a hurry.

I must have dozed off, lulled to sleep my the mechanical drone of the printer. I woke to a loud pounding. At first I thought the printer had run amok, but it seemed to be fine. In fact, it seemed to have completed its task. I was checking my watch, and staring out the window into the dusk in order to figure out how long I'd been out when the pounding started up again. My brain woke up enough to recognize that there was someone at the door. I slid up to the door and stuck my eye to the peephole.

A few years ago, it seems there was a lot of trouble in the Humanities Buildling with weirdos harrassing the female staff working late at night. In a fit of brilliance, the maintenance department installed peepholes in the doors of all the female members of the staff. I figured it was cheaper than neon and about as effective at pointing out the proper doors to the weirdos. Whatever the case, tonight I was grateful that there was a peephole in Quinn's door.

Maybe it was Guy, piped a little voice in my head. No such luck. What I saw through the fish eye lens was a man in a brown uniform. Campus Security.

"What is it?" I called through the door.

"Hmm mumbed a whummmed buidib," came the reply.

"I beg your pardon?" That's all I needed, an acid head security guard outside the door. He was starting his alien sentence over again when it hit me that I was still wearing my ear plugs. "Wait a second," I yelled, yanking the yellow foam pills out of my ears. "What did you say?"

"Just checking, ma'am. Someone reported seeing a stranger in the building, and I saw your light on so I thought I'd check to see if you needed an escort out of the building."

Just what I knew would happen to me in my wildest nightmares, I was going to be locked up in a building with a serial killer. I checked the printer. It was finished.

"Just a second," I yelped through the door. I yanked out the floppies, turned off the machinery and was halfway out in the hallway, clutching the manuscript under my arm, in ten seconds flat.

"Let me just check that I've got everything," I smiled at the guard, praying he didn't know Dr. Quinn on sight. I turned and gave a thorough glance over the office, making sure everything was as I'd found it in the morning. My eye caught sight of a pile of mail on Quinn's desk that I'd shuffled through but not paid much attention to earlier.

"Wait a second, could you," I smiled at the guard.

"Sure, but I'm going off shift now," he said with that added tone of belligerence high school graduates reserve for those of us who've thrown away monetary pursuits for a more esoteric quest.

"I won't be a sec," I said over my shoulder, dashing back into the room to pull something from Quinn's mail pile. Guy must have been emptying her pigeonhole in the main office. None of this was opened, and it was just as well. Among plastic bags containing the *Times Literary Supplement* and departmental fliers was a bright pink envelope I recognized in an instant. It was my letter to Ahlers' estate via McKendricks Publishers. What was it doing in Quinn's office?

The security guard coughed behind me. I stuffed the envelope into my pocket and turned back to him, pulling the office door locked behind me.

In five minutes I was on a bus home, feeling like Jack heading down the beanstalk. Sing, harp, sing.

Chapter 26

Why had McKendricks forwarded my request to Quinn? The only thing I could figure was that Quinn had been made executor of Ahlers' papers. Why she wouldn't have let her grad student know this little tidbit was beyond me. I knew she was cool toward me, but this was taking a lack of simpatico a little far in my books.

My irritating little inner voice piped up.

"You broke into her summer cottage, ransacked her office and have practically accused her of being a killer, and you're annoyed she hasn't shared Ahlers' papers with you?"

All right, all right, so I wound easily. All I knew was that Quinn's disregard for the virtue of sharing had wiped out any guilt I had felt about my puny crimes toward her. Reading Ahler's last novel was going to be especially sweet because I knew Quinn would writhe if she knew about it.

I was settled into the one comfy chair in the apartment, with the accordion of computer paper stacked on my knees when the phone rang. It was late. I wasn't expecting anyone. I was about to let the machine answer when I remembered that Guy was supposed to call. I raced to the phone, barking my leg against the doorknob as I rounded the corner.

"Hello?"

"Did you leave any signs that you were in there?"

"Hello Guy, nice to hear from you."

"Quick, Randy, I'm serious. Should I race over and tidy up, or what?"

"What's up? Of course I left it tidy. No one could tell there's been anyone in there but maybe you with the mail." Guy's voice didn't usually carry that much of a tone of panic in it. I was curious. "Why?"

"I got home about an hour ago, and there was a letter from Quinn in the mail. She's coming home earlier than expected. She'll be back on Wednesday. I just wanted to make sure that everything was tidy, because I have to spend the next two days down in Interlibrary Loans filling out forms."

"So there's no pressing need to get the wagons in a circle?"

"No, I guess not. It's just that I feel that everything gets so cloak-and-dagger when you get involved in things. Did you find what you were looking for?"

"Evidence that she's not gifted in the filing department, but aside from that not much."

"Oh well, I thought it might be worth a try."

"Yeah, well, thanks anyway."

"I guess I'll see you in a while."

"Yeah, right, Guy. Take care."

"You too, Randy. G'night."

"G'night."

I hung up and stared at the phone in front of me. Why had I lied to Guy? It was a reflex action, because consciously I had been planning on telling him about the manuscript. There had been something in his voice, something odd. It made me wonder again if he wasn't a little closer to his third reader than he had made out at first.

That was ridiculous. If he was Quinn's henchman, why would he have let me into her office? Quinn certainly wouldn't have wanted me there. Again I thanked the heavens I had been able to rescue the fuscia letter. I didn't need to telegraph my moves to Quinn anymore than I already had.

I moved back into the ersatz living room. There by the chair was a cup of decaf and three hundred pages worth of Pandora's box. Was I worried?

I smiled and went for it. You can't spend your life ruled by fairy tales and superstition. After all, three myths and you're out.

The first thing that struck me was that it was a mystery novel. I couldn't believe it at first, but as I turned the pages it came clear that the character Ophelia wasn't kidding when she introduced herself as a private eye. It was the first of Ahlers' novels to be written completely in the first person, and at first I wasn't sure if I liked the change.

About midway through the book I realized that not only was I enjoying myself, but that this was no ordinary mystery novel. If you can imagine Paul Quarrington getting together with Italo Calvino and reworking an idea by Dashiell Hammett, you'd have some idea of was I was talking about. There were mysteries within mysteries, and Ophelia wasn't much good as a private eye. In fact, she was making a much better victim in a Perils-of-Pauline sort of way. The evil characters kept splitting into twins, and as it got more confusing it also began to take on more and more character- istics of the old hard-boiled detective novels.

Ophelia wore white all the time. She had a theory that being very showy was in itself the best possible camouflage. No one would suspect her of being a private eye if she was so obvious. The trouble was everyone knew she was a private eye, they just didn't take her seriously.

Ahlers had turned the entire genre on its ear without malice. In fact, even though it was a complete parody of the form (even the title was a parody based on plucking and trussing the Maltese Falcon), I wouldn't be surprised if Feathers of Treasure wasn't at least nominated for an Arthur Ellis Award by the Crime Writers' of Canada.

I wondered what the academic circles were going to think of this shift in genre. I bet Quinn didn't like it. In fact, it made me chuckle out loud to imagine Quinn's reaction to this last book of Ahlers. My laughter died in the air as my thoughts actually shifted clear. Quinn's reaction to Ahlers' last novel might indeed be what motivated the word "last".

I grabbed my legal pad. Scribbling always helps me think. Quinn knew Ahlers. Quinn was making her academic reputation on Ahlers' back, in a manner of speaking. Quinn was finally getting some recognition in her field. Ahlers, her so-called friend, turns around and writes a mystery novel.

Quinn would be apoplectic. Suppose Ahlers had intended to write more mysteries, maybe even make Ophelia a series detective. It could be done, I supposed; maybe not quite Hercule Poirot, but sort of like Tom Berger's Russell Wren.

It could hamper Quinn's career a bit. She'd certainly have to branch into genre work, and then who knows, she'd have hordes of pimply honors students, whose only virtue was having seen every episode of Star Trek, wanting to do their tutorials with her on the grounds that she was sympathetic to popular literature. I was beginning to see grounds for murder, all right.

Okay, so Quinn reads Feathers of Treasure. She comes to all the same logical conclusions I had just outlined, so she murders Ahlers, becomes executor of Ahlers' papers, and sits on the new novel in order to maintain her ideal of a standard. I bought it as a motive, but I wasn't too sure the police would. I couldn't see them taking the "publish or perish", or in this case "publish and perish" mentality literally. Would anyone believe me? What I really needed was proof of the crime. Or a signed confession. I wasn't fussy.

Chapter 27

I woke up in a cold sweat on Monday morning.

I have always prided myself on bringing assignments in on time, no matter what. While it may mean a sleepless night or two, it also insures future business. Nobody wants to go searching for the freelancer they hired while technicians or typesetters twiddle their thumbs on the other end. There may be flashier writers in this business, but there aren't any more dependable.

And here it was Monday, and I had to have a chapter in to Quinn for Thursday.

I had to admit it was anti-climactic to be thinking about essay deadlines when there was a possible murder mystery to uncover, but on the other hand, I figured that even Miss Marple had to do her ironing on Tuesdays, so I might as well dig in and get to work instead of gripe about it.

Guy phoned just as the coffee was perking. He was a lot easier to put off than the thoughts of the mysterious mystery novel, but even so it took twenty minutes to tell him I wasn't interested in driving out to see buffalo in a paddock. I was laughing at his usual inanities as I got off the phone, but as I poured my coffee I started wondering why he was suddenly so fancy free. I thought he'd been slating a long stint in periodicals or something. I dragged myself over to my Kaypro and leaned forward to find the ON switch at the back. Pretty soon I'd forgotten Guy, Quinn and everything, including my cup of coffee which tasted horrible cold, in an attempt to pull my thoughts on regionality together.

The more I worked, the more I realized that this was going to be a down-to-the-wire job. No only was my pride a factor in all of this, I had to make this good enough to make Quinn believe I'd been working on it for the last two months. The last thing I needed was her suspecting that I'd instead been tracking her past and burglarizing her cabin or her office.

It was past nine in the evening on Wednesday when I hit the twenty page mark. I'd been over it so many times that my proofing the chapter would have been ridiculous. There was no one to call at this time of night, although Maureen probably would have proofed it out of the goodness of her heart. I figured a wisk through the spelling checker would do the trick.

Finally, at ten past eleven I was holding a printed copy of Chapter One. It wasn't the best thing I'd ever written, but it sure wasn't the worst thing ever written either. Quinn might find fault with the argument, but there was no way she could sink me on not knowing my material. I knew those books inside out. Upside down. Backwards. In fact, hypnotized, I might even be able to quote most of Ahlers' opus verbatim, that's so immersed I was in it.

And that's what was going to bring me closer to death than I'd like to come for another forty years, thank you.

Chapter 28

It was that stalemated, becalmed time of the year; the time that hits just around the tenth of August when it's too hot to party and too late to make travel plans and too close for comfort to all the deadlines you made in May. I had about twenty hours left to complete as a research assistant for Bella Spanner, Shakespeare scholar and Chairman of the department. R.A. work is never fun and rarely interesting but at least Dr. Spanner's requests seemed to have a purpose to them. She would leave detailed requests in my pigeonhole, and I'd go attempt to ferret out the information from the MLA.

It seems she had received rather ambiguous comments back from a reviewer when submitting her last article on the sonnets. They'd made some comparison to a fellow who'd made some comparison to Petrarch, but they'd neglected to give a reference. It fell to me to find everything the fellow had ever written to determine to which article the reviewer was referring.

I had a list of about nine titles dating back to 1968, which was the date of the fellow's dissertation. I know, I know, some people publish while still in grad school, but I figure these folk are aberations who just couldn't get dates. Besides, the MLA makes me sneeze. Armed with my meager list, I left Rutherford North and headed for the Periodical Library in Rutherford South.

I love the Periodical Library. For one thing, it's housed in the older part of the library and it makes me feel like I'm in an old Jimmie Stewart movie just walking through the doors. The marble stairs have grooves worn in them from seventy-odd years of academic trundling. The librarian's counter is made of old oak and the microfiche machines are tastefully hidden around the corner. As for the periodicals themselves, they are housed in rabbit warrens that you reach by climbing up and down narrow stairwells and sidling along ceiling-high metal stacks. Every time I came here I promised myself that I would drop by weekly to read the *Times Literary Supplement* or browse through old copies of *The New Yorker*. I never seem to get around to it, though. Somehow, once you left the Periodical Library, it vanished back into the mist like some sort of Brigadoon adjacent to Hub Mall, reappearing only when you had a specific article to find.

I'd found three of the rather ponderous looking journals on my list and decided to head upstairs for the fourth before I lined up to photocopy them for Dr. Spanner's files. I was busy juggling tomes so it wasn't until I was halfway into the tiny aisle that I realized I wasn't alone. I looked up, expecting to see a librarian or another grad student. Unless you had to be here, or suffered from sun allergies, no one would pick a day like this to visit the stacks. It wasn't a librarian and I guess melanoma fears are underrated in Alberta. I was alone in the stacks with Hilary Quinn.

My startled gasp sounded louder than it might have been. Perhaps it was an echo effect, or maybe I feared this woman I half suspected as a murderer more than I let on to myself. I found myself wishing it back, partially because it sounded so rude, and partially because it seemed to affirm something for Dr. Quinn. Something about me, and I wished to hell I could read what it was in her eyes.

"Dr. Quinn. I didn't expect to see you here. Well, I guess I didn't expect to see anyone here." Oh great, my mental editor sighed, when cornered, ramble. Quinn seemed to take stock of my discomfiture and moved closer to take advantage of it.

"This is a fortuitous meeting, Randy. I was thinking of setting up a session to discuss the implications of your chapter."

"Oh really? I didn't expect you to get onto it so quickly. I've hardly begun the next one."

"That's handy. I wanted to talk to you before you went too far down the wrong track."

The wrong track? What the hell was she talking about? I knew it wasn't my best work, but it did lay out the basis of what we'd discussed and agreed upon in our prior meetings. It was a little dry, but that surely seemed to be de rigeur considering the construct. After all, academic writing was hardly edge-of-the-chair stuff.

"You seem to have readjusted your thinking on the concept of Ahlers' trilogy of place, I notice."

There was something in her tone of voice that was making me sweat, but I still couldn't figure out what she was getting at. Trilogy of place? A warning light was just starting to glow in my head, and when she started to speak again the sirens came on.

"How did you get hold of the fourth book?"

"Fourth book?" I stuttered. For a second I felt thrilled and justified in my reasoning until I realized that I didn't need this kind of confirmation from Quinn. After all, it had been her computer I'd robbed it from. Still, how did she know I knew? My thoughts must have flashed across my face, because she laughed -- grimly.

"You mixed up the character names in your chapter. It happens all the time when working closely with more than one novel, especially when the characters are all fabrications of the same author. I find myself mixing up Isabel and Andrea at times. But you left yourself open when you mistakenly refer to Eleanor as Ophelia. Really. How did you find out about Ophelia?"

I'm used to thinking on my feet. Years of freelance interviewing and a session of freshman teaching had inured me to off-the-wall and trick questions. Still, how do you lie convincingly with your hand caught in the cookie jar? She knew, because of my weary brain doing lousy editing, that I had seen Feathers of Treasure. Where could I have seen it without being charged with a felony? I tried to paste on a smile to couch the bluff I was about to try.

"I have a friend at McKendricks who let me peek."

It took her less than a second to take in what I'd said and call me on it.

"You're lying. McKendricks has never seen the fourth manuscript. I suppose the ins and outs of your knowledge aren't important, but what is important to me is how much you know. Your curiosity might be very dangerous, for both of us."

Any doubts I'd had about her murdering Ahlers faded to black. She appeared to me there as the most cold-blooded mammal I'd ever seen. With that knowledge, a funny sort of calm settled over me, otherwise I'd never have asked her my next question.

"When did you decide to kill her?"

Quinn looked at me and laughed. It was an eerie laugh, part mockery and part crazy.

"Margaret? Oh I always knew she'd have to die."

I've heard about people that can talk terrorists out of planes, and jumpers off bridges and crazies out of their weapons. People like that must have some innate grace that overtakes them in moments of crisis. Having confronted such a critical moment I now know one thing; I'm not that sort of person. Dropping three volumes of *The International Symposium of Petrarchan Studies*, I turned and ran with Dr. Hilary Quinn at my heels.

Chapter 29

I dashed out of South Rutherford Library with the knowledge that at least one hound of hell was behind me. I could hear her heels clattering on the marble steps and she was hissing my name. It just goes to show how deeply the training not to shout in libraries is imbedded in our psyches. Murder was one thing, but shouting in libraries was still off limits. Outside, I turned automatically south toward the bus stop. I wasn't sure how close Quinn was behind me and I didn't want to take the time to check.

My running must have struck some prehistoric sympathetic chord in the lone bus driver there, because he paused to let me on before pulling away in one graceful motion. Fumbling with my wallet, I spotted Quinn standing at the receding curb, squinting into the sunlight to read the number of the bus.

The thought that she knew where I was headed made me shudder, and was closely followed by the the thought that she was one up on me. I had no idea what bus I was on.

"Where does this bus go?" I asked, over the clatter of the nickles and quarters cascading into the change box. The bus driver seemed to think my question absurd. After all, how many people rush for buses in the generic?

"West Edmonton Mall," he growled, as if I should have been able to assume this from the tilt of his cap. I thanked him, and stumbled back on the moving vehicle to find a perch.

West Edmonton Mall. This bus would go past my place on the way to the megamall, but I was sure Quinn would know my address, or have easy access to it. I didn't want to be cornered in my little basement suite that had only one entrance past the furnace and laundry room. My copy of Ahlers' unpublished last novel was there on the kitchen table, and all my cue cards would clue Quinn in to my activities, but she already knew that I knew enough to need silencing. I shook my head to clear the gothic thoughts that seemed so incongruous on a lazy August day in suburban Edmonton. Hilary Quinn, a respected scholar at the University, out to murder one of her graduate students? It didn't sound credible. I remembered the chill feeling of dread when I was alone with her in the Periodical stacks. I didn't want to be alone with her again. I'd take my chances at the Mall.

I've never understood the urge to hide away from people in unpopulated areas. People tend to stick out, rather than blend into nature. My best chance of anonymity was in the biggest crowd I could find, and if that crowd was anywhere in Edmonton, it would be at the Mall.

I got off the bus at the terminus and hurried through the parkade to the Zellers door. I figured I'd need a different shirt, since my aqua striped top was a little too distinctive, and would be what Quinn was looking for. I rifled through the first rack of t-shirts I came to, and picked out a black short-sleeved shirt with no advertising on it. I hate paying to be a sandwich board for a band or a cartoon figure on principle, and now I needed to fade into the scenery without any message that would blare out and make me memorable to sales clerks or easy pickings for murderers. I paid cash and hurried to the public washroom near the skating rink to bite off the sales ticket and whip on the shirt. It was a little loose, but I figured that was better than skin-tight. I pulled the elastic out of the French braid that had become my trademark since salon prices had skyrocketed, and finger combed my hair around my shoulders. I stuffed my shirt in the Zellers bag, and froze. Someone was coming into the washroom. Only when the next stall door banged shut did I creep out of my cell.

My heart stopped again as I tried to leave the washroom. My strongest urge was to hole up, not to be seen, but I knew that I'd be crazy to sit and wait here. It's one thing to see two teenage girls hanging around in a mall washroom, quite another for a lone thirty-year old. If Quinn didn't find me, I'd likely be reported. I had to keep on the move.

It's all well and good to hide in a crowd, but I couldn't stand the thought that Quinn was somewhere in this crowd, too, or would be soon, and I could just as easily tread on her toe as avoid her. I had to find a place to see without being seen first. I also had to sit down and think. I couldn't run forever. If only the panic could subside, I might be able to see a plan. At this point, all I wanted was a plan to save my own skin. Margaret Ahlers was already dead, there was nothing to be done for her.

I bought a coffee at the food fair next to Fantasyland and sat as near as I could to the back wall. I could cover both entrances from my vantage point, and make a beeline for either direction. Sitting among the tourists, tired shoppers and teenagers calmed me down a bit. Everything was so ordinary. In a way, that was the most macabre thing about the whole flight from the library. It was so clean and bright and non-threatening. Sort of like the Bates Motel the morning after.

I noticed a kid with curly blond hair and thought about Guy. Could I trust him enough to tell him where I was? What was his connection to all of this mess anyway? Why had he tried to get me off campus today? Did Quinn know about our collusion, or was it collusion?

Call me a hopeless romantic, but intuitively I couldn't accept Guy's involvement as some sort of spy attached to me. For one thing, Quinn had no reason to suspect my motives up till my lousy Freudian slip in my chapter. Freud now had even more to answer for. It occured to me that if Guy wasn't in cahoots with Quinn, she would soon twig to how I got hold of Ahlers' manuscript. Guy had the keys to her office. Guy didn't know what I'd found there, because I'd held back on the information. If Guy was innocent, I'd made him a sitting duck. I had to get hold of him.

I checked the scene before I got up to stow my coffee cup and find a phone. This would be the dangerous part. All the phone kiosks were located in central areas in the middle of the concourse. I made sure I had quarters in my hand and was jingling them like worry beads as I made my way out into the middle of the mall.

I tried him at home. No answer. I tried the general office. The secretaries hadn't seen him in today, and no, I didn't wish to leave a message. I didn't want any sort of trail for Quinn to follow from me to him. I hit the payphone in frustration. Where the hell was he? Had he really gone to Elk Island Park on a whim? Did that mean he was safely out of all this?

I don't know why I dialled the number to Quinn's office. Maybe I was still fearful of a conspiracy with Guy. Maybe I just wanted to place her logistically. If she was there answering her phone, she couldn't be stalking me with a butcher knife. A mixture of relief and horror flooded through me when her voice came on the line. I didn't say anything.

"Hello?" she repeated. She waited a beat or three and then said, "Miranda?"

I must have breathed idiosyncratically, because she went on with certitude.

"Miranda, we have to talk. I'm sure you'll want some sort of explanation, and I suppose, under the circumstances, you're entitled to one. I'm still not sure how you obtained access to the manuscript, but I assume you've read it." There was a silence from me, which she took as confirmation.

"Well, I'm sure you understand that after this novel, there would be no more need for Ahlers. Can't you see that it was optimum for me to silence her before her work took on second-rate signs or reduced in strength? Look what happened to Tennessee Williams in later life. He should have been stopped after *The Rose Tattoo*."

I couldn't believe the cold-blooded way she was talking. Silencing a writer before they lost it artistically? I've heard of censorship, but this was really taking it to the limit.

She went on.

"Perhaps if we could talk, I could explain. It would do me good, probably, to talk about it to someone. Would you come to the office tonight, about seven? I'm sure I could make you understand my position."

"Dr. Quinn," I finally said. "I've been to Trumpeter Lake. I don't think there's anything you need to tell me."

Her voice changed somehow. I realized with hindsight that she'd been pleading with me, and she was through. The supplication, what little she'd been able to muster, was gone from her next words.

"You've been up north. I see. Well, perhaps you're right. Perhaps there is nothing more to say."

The dial tone began to buzz in my ear.

Chapter 30

I made my way back to my neighbourhood with my mind on Nancy Drew. She always got clobbered in the line of busybodiness, but she managed to spring back time after time and get the baddie. Maybe it wasn't possible to ferret out truth without getting bludgeoned. Of course, I was alone in this venture, I thought, as I rounded the house to get to the back door leading to my suite. Nancy always had her ivy league boyfriend to get her out of her jams. What was his name?

"Ned Nickerson!"

"I beg your pardon?" Guy unfolded himself from his perch on the back steps. "I know it's been a couple of days, but surely you could make a pretense of remembering my name?"

I was so glad to see him that I gave him a hug that neither of us were expecting, and we almost toppled back onto the steps. Guy regained his composure and balance first.

"Really, Randy, what would the landlords say? Why don't we go inside and you can demonstrate how glad you are to see me at our leisure."

Relief at seeing him turned quickly into anger, the sort mothers demonstrate to kids who've lost themselves in grocery stores.

"Where the hell have you been? Do you realize what I've been through, and trying to call you, and..." My hand was shaking so much I couldn't direct the key into the Yale on the back door. Guy took the keys out of my hand like the men did in fifties movies and soon had me sitting at my kitchen table.

I stared at my knees while he busied himself around, and the next thing I knew I was drinking very sugary hot tea.

"Ew. What's this?"

"The only part I remember from my St. John's Ambulance course. Sugar in the tea for shock. I'm assuming it's shock, and not the d.t.'s you're exhibiting. Where have you been?"

"West Edmonton Mall."

"Well, then it's shock all right."

I laughed, in spite of everything. Guy looked so concerned, and helpful and downright nice that I decided at that moment that he couldn't be some sort of evil cohort of Quinn's. Maybe it was just that I was too tired to go on suspecting people. Ahlers had been murdered, I'd been chased, I'd been forced to wear a Zellers T-shirt; it was all getting too much for me.

"I suppose you want to hear the story thus far."

"If you're up to it."

"I think I'll go mad if I don't talk about it."

Guy sat on one of my teetery chrome chairs while I told him of finding the hidden diskettes, and my forwarded letter from the publisher designating Quinn as the executor of Ahlers' papers, and the discovery of the fourth novel. I continued by explaining my slip in nomenclature, and Quinn's admission of murder, the chase to the bus and my terror at the mall. Piece by piece it didn't sound like much, but connected in the torrent spilling over my tonsils it all seemed to add up and Guy looked like he agreed with me. At least he looked captivated. Maybe it was my T-shirt.

"And then she hung up on you?"

"Click. Final."

"But what did she mean by there's nothing more to say? What do you think she was going to explain to you in her office?"

I shrugged.

"Her relationship with Ahlers, I guess."

"But what about her relationship with Ahlers?"

"Guy, it's obvious. She and Ahlers were lovers. Ahlers was the creative writer, Quinn the academic. Sounds like a love-hate relationship to begin with. Real Eleanor and Marie stuff, if you think about it. Anyway, Ahlers allows Quinn first crack at her work, probably even before the proofs stage, so that Quinn can get the jump on anyone else in the academic market. Then, when the books are published, Quinn moves into the fore with her critical work on the novels."

"But why kill the goose that's laying the golden egg?"

"Because the fourth novel, the one as yet unpublished, is a detective novel. It's a brilliant detective novel, sort of a Nick and Nora meet Garcia Marquez, but a detective novel. Don't you see? All that territory staked on the next Margaret Laurence, or Margaret Atwood, and she turns into Margaret Millar?"

"I don't know; there's something missing in the argument."

"What?"

"I'm not sure. Why would Ahlers write a detective novel under her own name if she was concerned about her lover's critical reputation?"

"Maybe they'd fought. Maybe Quinn killed her because she'd ditched Quinn."

"Or maybe Quinn ditched her and so she meant to get back at her by writing a sub-literary text."

"Then why show it to Quinn? Why not just publish and laugh?"

"Maybe she just died naturally, and the papers went to Quinn as executor from an unchanged will."

"No." I banged my tea mug on the table for emphasis. "I may know nothing else about this whole mess, but I do know one thing right from the horse's mouth. Hilary Quinn killed Margaret Ahlers. Maybe it was a lover's quarrel. Maybe it was jealousy from a writer manque. Maybe she did it to edit her permanently. I know she did it, she told me as much. If I want to find out why, there's only one thing to do."

"And what's that?"

"Meet with Quinn at seven tonight."

"You're seriously thinking of bearding a murderer in her den?"

"I have to, Guy. The story's not over till it's over."

"Some stories are perfectly fine without closure, you know."

There was more than theoretical argument showing on Guy's face. He was worried about my safety, but I'd somehow moved beyond fear into the realm of pure curiosity. Fore-warned as I was, Quinn couldn't hurt me, and I even had the presence of mind to get the last word in with Guy. I grinned at him.

"Get thee behind me, Robbe-Grillet. You're talking here to the last Balzacian reader."

Chapter 31

The Humanities Building was locked at six on summer evenings but I was armed with my pass key and the thought that Campus Security was out there, somewhere. Guy had refused to let me tackle Quinn solo, but had agreed to remain in the Grad Lounge while I kept my rendezvous. It made things easier knowing there was help within screaming distance, but not much. For all my bravado earlier, I was getting spooked. Guy had told me he'd wait half an hour, and then come in metaphorical guns blazing. I took what comfort I could in, that knowledge.

There was no air moving in the building, and the banners that looked so cheerful hanging among the skylights at ten in the morning were mildly malevolent in the dusky light. It was the same feeling I got when visiting the Glenbow Museum's military gallery. I was obviously in a great state of mind to see Dr. Quinn.

"Come in," was the command elicited from my hesitant knock on her office door. Quinn was expecting me. She sat behind her desk like a besieged zealot. The visitor's chair was centered in the remaining floor space. I half expected arc lights to blaze into my face as I sat down. What the hell was I doing here?

"Thank you for keeping this appointment. I wasn't sure you would come."

"I wasn't sure I would either, but I thought I should get all my facts straight before I,... before I do anything."　I found myself stumbling over my words. What was I going to do with this information? Go to the police? The Dean of Arts?

"I suppose you'll be eager to publish, and I would rather you got all your facts straight, as you say. I suppose it's the scholar's dilemma; does one bluster and deny in this situation, or determine the accuracy of the presentation against one?"

I was stunned. Here was a woman on the brink of jail, and all she was worried about was getting quoted correctly. What the hell was she talking about? What did she assume I was going to publish, anyway? This was turning into a seminar instead of the showdown I'd anticipated. Of course, I don't really have that much experience with murderers, but this wasn't at all what I'd expected. I decided to blunder into the fog.

"We are talking about the murder of Margaret Ahlers?"

To my surprise, Quinn laughed. It wasn't an attractive laugh, but then I didn't have much of a basis of comparison considering I'd hardly ever even seen her crack a smile before.

"You sound like Conan Doyle's mother. No, of course not; I'm speaking about the creation of Margaret Ahlers." My face must have betrayed me, because this time Quinn did more than chuckle.

"Oh ho, now I understand! You have been cast as a modern Don Quixote, Miranda. You are out to avenge the death of a fiction. I'm sorry to have to tell you that your giant is a windmill."

"What are you talking about?" I asked her, but a glimmer of the truth was beginning to take form even before she spoke.

"I assumed you knew the truth when you spoke of Trumpeter Lake. I thought you'd found the dresses and the dummy."

"The dummy?"

"I had a dressmaker's dummy there. I'd put flashy clothes on it, and situate it around the cottage and the grounds to get people to assume there were two women up there instead of just me."

I thought about Dot stumbling over the L word.

"It worked. I heard about the two ladies who came every summer. You and your shadowy lover."

"My lover? How wonderful. I wasn't sure my ingenuous neighbours would make that connection. No wonder I never got any nosy visitors tripping over!"

"Why go to all the bother of creating a second woman?"

"I needed the solitude to get the most work done I could, and in case it became necessary, I needed a possibility of Ahlers to exist. I see it was necessary; you must have been quite industrious to follow such a meager trail."

Finally, I was getting some praise from my advisor. It wasn't quite what I'd had in mind, but it kept me in a state of shocked silence nonetheless. Quinn noticed it, and continued in a professorial tone. It occured to me, somewhat irrelevantly, that she must be a pretty good lecturer.

"There never was a Margaret Ahlers, Miranda. I created her and then disposed of her when she had fulfilled my purpose."

"You wrote the novels?"

"You still don't understand, do you? It was the only way I had to make it in this business. We hate to call it a business, but behind the ivy covered walls is an industry like any other. To get tenure and advance, you must publish. To publish, you need a topic, preferably a topic no one else has covered with their own minutiae. There aren't that many topics to go around, in case you hadn't noticed."

The trouble was I had noticed. Why else had I been so eager to tackle Ahlers? Because she was fantastic, or because she was virgin territory? Quinn was convincing, but one thing just didn't make sense.

"But if you could write like Ahlers, I mean like you did, why didn't you publish them under your own name? Why hide from that talent?"

"You mean, why hide from the glory and the honour of being a lauded writer?"

I nodded.

"All I have ever wanted to be was an academic. Always. Even before I came to university, I knew that someday I'd be here, where I belong. Not all critics are failed writers, although that's what most people assume. Some of us revel in the exploration of the words of others; what those words say about the authors, the readers, and our civilization. I had to get into the enclave. Maybe it was cheating, but I knew that this is where I belonged, where I could function properly."

She looked around her office, this niche she'd carved for herself in the fortress of great minds.

"I was granted tenure six months ago. I no longer need to be novel, just insightful. I don't need Ahlers anymore."

"Then why the mystery novel?"

"Oh, is that worrying you? I was playing around with the story when I got wind of the tenure committee's decision. Since I had the time, I finished it. Perhaps it was the hint of skullduggery behind my own actions that inspired it. I don't suppose I'll have it published by Ahlers posthumously; it doesn't really fit the oeuvre, does it?"

I wasn't afraid of her any longer. She inspired disbelief, and a bit of pity, but no fear. It came to me that, if what she said was true, that I held her future in my hands like Alice's pack of cards.

"If I expose this, what will happen to you?"

She returned to reality, and stared at me.

"If you publish what you know, my career ceases to be. This would not be entirely your fault. I knew the risks involved when I conceived of the short cut. I won't beg you not to tell, I've never begged for anything. I'll have to wait and see what you decide. Just remember, what you decide affects your windmills too."

I was being dismissed. I left her sitting behind her hard-won desk, staring at the McNaught painting telling her just how far she'd come. The meeting had taken twenty minutes. I turned down the hall toward the Grad Lounge to pick up Sancho Panza.

Chapter 32

Guy and I were up most of the night going over everything we knew and all that I'd learned from Quinn that evening. I'd sworn him to secrecy, at least until I'd decided what to to about it. Damn Quinn anyway, for abdicating responsibility.

"I don't know where the conundrum lies?" Guy continued with the argument he'd been promoting for the last hour or so. "This could set you up for life. You expose the greatest literary hoax since the Desiderata. It nets you a thesis, a mass market book, and maybe even an interview with Vicky Gabereau. What's the problem?"

"The Desiderata, that's the problem."

"I don't follow you."

"If I expose the hoax, and really, how much of a hoax is it, then not considering what happens to Quinn's career, what happens to Ahlers' work?"

"You mean Quinn's work."

"No, I mean Ahlers' work. Look at history. What about Ossian? Beethoven was supposed to have loved him, but now all we think about is that it was a Romantic hoax, not what great poetry it was. Or Chatterton. Sure, his story gets Ackroyd on the Booker shortlist, but does anyone read his poetry for its value as poetry, or just as a clever fake?"

"But doesn't Quinn deserve the credit of being the one to perpetrate such a magnificent hoax?"

"She doesn't want credit, or she'd have signed her name in the first place. Look, I'm not worried about Quinn. Let

Quinn look out for herself. I'm worried about Ahlers. We need those novels as novels. They should be read on their own merit, not treated as artifacts. Artificial artifacts."

"So what are you saying?"

"I guess I'm saying that I'm not going to do anything about it."

"What about the next eager bloodhound that comes along? Someone's going to come up with the goods; why shouldn't it be you?"

"Because I have to live with myself." I shook my head, and shrugged myself into motion. "I'm beat. I need about twenty hours of sleep and then some. Go home, Guy. I'll call you when I get back in gear."

"I'll come and get you for a sinfully large breakfast at Uncle Albert's."

I gave him a quick kiss.

"Yum. And, Guy, I know you don't understand, or approve, but thanks for the solidarity."

No problem, Comrade. You know me, always one to play by the rules."

I went to sleep thinking about Guy who didn't really understand me, and Quinn who did; and of a shadowy woman in a flowery dress standing on the other side of the lake. No matter what Guy or Quinn thought, she did exist, and it was she to whom I owed my loyalty.

The phone woke me. It was Guy.

"I thought I said I'd call you. What time is it, anyway?"

"Randy, I'm over at the Department. I thought you ought to know. Dr. Quinn killed herself last night. Here, in her office. Randy?"

I hung up the phone. There was nothing to say.

As a detective, I'd been worse than E.C. Bentley's Trent. The most you could say for me was that I'd been persistent. And finally, after all the digging, I'd succeeded where a lot of literary critics fail. I'd found the body. But the blood was on my hands.

Chapter 33

I spent the morning with Guy at the Department. The police were there, but since Quinn had left a note explaining her motives as stress-related job pressures, they didn't seem too interested in questioning hordes of people. She'd had a gun, something I hadn't found while searching her office, but maybe it hadn't been there then.

I needed to walk. I found myself on Saskatchewan Drive, looking back at the Humanities Building and counting off the windows to find hers. It was appropriate for her to have died in her office; she'd spent her whole life getting there.

What could I have said to her to assure her of my silence? Maybe nothing. Maybe Guy was right and Quinn had realized it. One day, someone would discover the hoax and blow her tidy life out of the water. At least now, Ahlers would have a chance, and Quinn could maintain some dignity.

I thought about my thesis, which seemed inordinately anti-climatic. Should I finish it? I could see myself second-guessing myself, and having to obscure my research to muddy the trail from Ahlers to Quinn. Was it worth it? I considered the options, and then decided against it. Getting out of here and back in the swim of things would be healthier. Quinn had insisted on calling me Miranda. Well, I'd take my cue from Prospero's daughter, and drown the book.

Near the Faculty Club, I heard some caterwauling coming from one of the trees. A small cat was surrounded by jeering magpies. One of them kept jumping closer along the cat's limb, taunting the supposed superior on the food chain. I smiled as I counted the magpies, a habit I'd gotten into. One, two, three, four, five, six, seven. Seven for a story never told. I gave the tree a mock salute and headed off in the general direction of the library.